LET THE REASON BE
LOVE

Author, screenwriter and columnist, **Tuhin A. Sinha** is acknowledged among the most prolific Indian writers.

Having authored titles like *That Thing Called Love*—a bestselling romance novel, *The Edge of Desire*—a socio-political thriller, *Daddy: The Birth of a Father*—India's first parenting book from a father's perspective, he is widely known for his knack to experiment with new genres. *Let the Reason Be Love* is Tuhin's eighth book.

At present, he is a consultant with Reliance Broadcast, in charge of new programming initiatives for their TV channel, Big Magic.

LET THE REASON BE
LOVE

TUHIN A. SINHA

RUPA

Published by
Rupa Publications India Pvt. Ltd 2015
7/16, Ansari Road, Daryaganj
New Delhi 110002

Sales Centres:

Allahabad Bengaluru Chennai
Hyderabad Jaipur Kathmandu
Kolkata Mumbai

Copyright © Tuhin A. Sinha 2015

This is a work of fiction. Names, characters, places and incidents are either the product of the author's imagination or are used fictitiously and any resemblance to any actual person, living or dead, events or locales is entirely coincidental.

All rights reserved.
No part of this publication may be reproduced, transmitted, or stored in a retrieval system, in any form or by any means, electronic, mechanical, photocopying, recording or otherwise, without the prior permission of the publisher.

ISBN: 978-81-291-3474-5

First impression 2015

10 9 8 7 6 5 4 3 2 1

The moral right of the author has been asserted.

Printed by Thomson Press India Ltd., Faridabad

This book is sold subject to the condition that it shall not, by way of trade or otherwise, be lent, resold, hired out, or otherwise circulated, without the publisher's prior consent, in any form of binding or cover other than that in which it is published.

*To the utopian idea of
falling in love all over again*

One

> *Pleasure of love lasts but a moment.*
> *Pain of love lasts a lifetime.*
> —BETTE DAVIS

February 2014

At 6.20 a.m., as dawn broke, allowing a faint light to dissipate the darkness, it lent a pristine, beatific still feel to the turquoise waters of the exotic Palolem beach in South Goa. At that moment, everything around seemed a picture of majestic serenity. Everything, except an elevated beach hut, just about a hundred metres away from the shore!

This hut was the venue of an intense carnal engagement between a young married couple, Rishaan Sahay and Kiara Sen. Rishaan held Kiara from behind, kissing her generously from the back of her neck, right down to her lower back. They had been into the act for almost half an hour, a time good enough to culminate. But something seemed amiss that day. A sleepy Rishaan was not able to retain the momentum for long, compelling them to postpone the climax twice.

Kiara knew Rishaan was stressed. The last one year, since

they had started trying to conceive, had been tough on their sex life. While they certainly indulged in the act more often, the consciousness about the 'right dates', the positions and the attendant anxieties about the end result, had taken away much of the sheen from the act. It seemed more mechanical now, as compared to the spontaneous ecstasy it used to be.

Had it been another situation, Kiara would have perhaps told Rishaan to chill and let go. But letting go was not an option anymore. In fact, the couple had been suspecting fertility issues. The Goa sojourn, meant to be their baby-making holiday, was their last attempt to make things happen the natural way before exploring other alternatives. They had already made love eight times in the last three days. And yet when Kiara felt that faint-ovulatory-pain-kind-of-sensation an hour ago, she wasted no time in waking Rishaan up and engaging him in the act once again.

On sensing Rishaan's nonchalance, Kiara quickly jogged her memory to recall what could still conjure passion between them. She knew the few hours succeeding ovulation were critical for conceiving. Kiara mounted atop Rishaan, sensuously swabbing his upper body with her breasts, while intensely caressing his crucial parts with her hand and locking lips all at once. In less than two minutes, the result was achieved. Rishaan entered Kiara fairly hard, with her still on top. The conjured passion made him reverse the position and roll her down in zest, with the penetration still intact. When the climax was finally attained both loosened up with a sense of relief that had 'hope' written all over it.

In less than five minutes, Kiara had dozed off, while Rishaan was swamped by a gamut of memories that kept him away from slumber. As he watched Kiara sleep in his arms, he couldn't help but wonder how much she had changed in the four years since their first meeting. From the fiercely-independent, career-centric, sexy woman she used to be, she now lived a relatively timid life that revolved majorly around Rishaan and her craving to be a mother.

Was Kiara the same woman whom Rishaan had fallen for? Well, he was never sure if he had actually fallen for her. Or perhaps, was it her transformation along the way that had made him love her as much as he did today?

Life, Rishaan inferred, seldom provided clear answers to her conundrums.

Two

We met for a reason.
Either you're a blessing or a lesson.

February 2010

What is it that brings two strangers together and makes them fall in love? Are people always meant to fall in love the way they do or is it a common void in their lives that propels them to go for the first suitable stranger who comes along?

This conundrum will perhaps exist as long as people continue to fall in love.

All those who have lived in Mumbai would vouch for how tedious it used to be to travel from Andheri West to Andheri East, especially during peak rush hours. Both areas combined together are about as large as the size of a city in Europe. The railway lines bifurcating the two parts resulted in an elongated road route full of traffic jams and chaos. This was of course before the Versova–Ghatkopar Metro started in July 2014 and decimated the distance.

It thus took Rishaan almost an hour to travel from his

rented apartment in Seven Bungalows to the Star TV office, which then used to be at Sakinaka. He spent this time listening to the FM channels on the music system of his second-hand Honday City, R.D. Burman's renditions from the seventies being his favourite. And along with it, he would invariably be thinking about the episodes of the two daily soaps that he was supervising as the channel's executive producer. At times, the traffic was so sluggish that he managed to read the printout of a full episode's screenplay, waiting at the seven odd traffic signals that dotted his route.

On one such February morning, which incidentally was also his last week at Star, while driving to office, Rishaan seemed uncharacteristically aloof. This led to him nearly ramming his car into an auto rickshaw; thankfully he was saved by a whisker from being hit by a BEST bus. Hating himself for the condition he had brought himself to be in, Rishaan consciously switched off of the radio and kept the printouts in his bag. His thoughts revolved around a heartbreak. Rishaan was seething for being hurt and taken for a ride by the girl he had begun to fancy a future with.

Shama Pervez was Rishaan's senior at Star TV. She was in a long-distance relationship with a man called Hanif, whom she had known since college. In fact, both their families were also well known to each other. In their decade-long relationship, Hanif and she had broken off twice, but patched up within a few months on both occasions. Hanif was in the US for the last one year, pursuing his PhD. They chatted on Skype every second day, enabling them to feel as connected as ever.

When Rishaan joined Star two years ago, Shama was his

senior colleague on the two shows that he was given to handle. In the process, Rishaan learnt a great deal from Shama. The two would spend a good amount of time discussing work and subsequently, as they became friends, their personal issues. Shama was a warm person, traditional, caring and extremely sincere with her work. She looked quite beautiful with her long, auburn hair, even though she was a bit plump. Knowing that Rishaan lived alone, she would get him home-cooked breakfast. This camaraderie led to a thicker bond with Rishaan, who gradually became her confidant and a very close friend.

As Rishaan got to know Shama better, he discovered that Shama and Hanif were together more out of a safe habit than out of volition. Things certainly weren't hunky-dory between them. After Hanif decided to settle in the US, a prospect Shama was not in favour of, things had begun to drift apart. Eight months ago, after a prolonged phase of skirmishes and misunderstandings, they formally broke off. Rishaan was aware of this development. He made use of the opportunity to really support her through it. And three months later he took Shama out on their first official date. Another couple of months later, he proposed to her. Shama accepted reluctantly, not unaware that her family may not approve of the match easily. And just three weeks ago, Shama suddenly called off the relationship after she patched up with Hanif and decided to go off to the US immediately.

This morning, when Rishaan checked his mail, he was in for a ruder shock. Shama had sought forgiveness from him and informed that Hanif and she were getting married in the next two months.

Rishaan thought it was okay to fall in and out of love.

That didn't seem unnatural in the transient world that they were living in. What hurt him was that terrible feeling of having been used. Even if it were not done unintentionally, it was now clear that Shama had never moved on from Hanif. In hindsight, her brief involvement with Rishaan seemed an arduous effort to convince herself that she could love another man, a thing she perhaps knew deep within, she couldn't. So, Rishaan was her experiment with truth! The tragedy for Rishaan was that he couldn't even vent out his angst on her; she was just too lovable for that. All he could do what rue his luck.

As Rishaan battled the chaos in his head, his car suddenly stopped. 'Gosh!' The petrol tank was empty. He wondered how he could be so unmindful. The cumulative crooning of horns from behind made him seek help from an auto driver having his chai by the roadside stall. Together, they dragged his car to the side of the road.

After five minutes and five calls from his boss, Mita reminded him that he still had to finalize the next two months' broad stories for both his shows before quitting. For Rishaan, more than the stress of completing the assignment, it it felt good to think that this was the last week his 42-year-old single, tomboyish boss could call him at inopportune moments.

He quickly opted for what seemed a more practical thing to do—hire an auto, rush to the office, and then later try and leave early and fix his car.

♦

As bad timing would have it, for quite a while Rishaan couldn't find an empty auto that would go to Sakinaka. And then when he got one to stop, he realized that a strikingly good-looking girl standing close by had simultaneously called for the same auto. From the mischievous glint in the auto driver's eyes, it was obvious that he'd prefer stealing glimpses of a 5 feet 9 inches, well-toned, pretty looking, dusky babe on his rear view mirror, than hosting an average-looking man. Given that Rishaan was running late, he was in no mood to relent either.

'Kahan jaana hai?' the auto driver reached out to the babe, ignoring Rishaan consciously.

'Sakinaka,' she answered.

'Baittho madam.'

'Excuse me, can we share the ride please? I'll pay the whole fare.' Rishaan asked the girl.

The girl nodded, gracefully yet detached. From the auto driver's expression, it was apparent he did not appreciate her generosity.

No sooner had the auto journey begun than the girl got a call on her cell.

'Yes, this is Kiara Sen,' she answered.

'Sorry, I am not considering any retirement plans. Please don't call me again,' she replied tersely, disconnecting the bank agent's unsolicited sales call.

Rishaan found this girl rather attractive. She seemed to have great features; though he was yet to see her eyes as they were covered with large-sized brown glares. But what he liked more about her was the cold confidence in her husky voice and the rationed use of words. From his first impression about her, she looked super confident. Within moments, though, this notion was dispelled as she was to reveal her emotionally fragile side

Kiara got a call from her best buddy, apparently from Canada. And with her, she seemed a different person, as fallible as any other girl her age.

'...Diya, he was such a rogue, I tell you...I can't understand how someone can lie like that... I feel so cheated and used... Gosh! I can never trust a man again...not in this life.'

Rishaan would have liked to hear her more but an important call from his colleague took all his attention. And by the time he was done, Kiara too was off the phone.

'Is it alright if I smoke?' she asked.

Rishaan nodded.

She lit her cigarette with the elan of a habitual smoker, and then took off her glares. From the side glances and then a more direct one which Rishaan managed through looking at the auto driver's rear view mirror, he felt reassured that he was seated next to a bombshell. She had large, deep, sensuous eyes, with just those peculiar cuts around them that made him think she was from one of the eastern states.

Rishaan was tempted to broach a conversation. But seeing her aloof, smoking and gazing aimlessly at the road outside, he found it unwarranted. Rishaan, anyway, was not sure if he would meet her ever again.

'Left mein rok dena.' Rishaan guided the auto driver.

The auto stopped with a jerk, pulling Kiara back from her thoughts.

'Is this the Star office?' she asked Rishaan.

Rishaan nodded as he took out a five hundred rupee note.

Kiara instead managed the exact change of Rs85, making Rishaan feel a bit embarrassed.

He wondered what brought her to the Star office. And

before he could ask, Kiara got another call on her cell. Seeing her deep in conversation, Rishaan found it a bit odd to be hanging around her. He proceeded inside, only to be coerced by his inquisitiveness to have an introduction, and stopped midway in the lobby. He kept fiddling with his phone, until he saw her walk in. Kiara proceeded towards the lift with Rishaan following close behind her.

They entered the lift. As the door closed behind them, Kiara realized that the guy next to her was the auto-mate. 'Hi.' both greeted each other simultaneously with the warmth of a prior acquaintance.

'Rishaan Sahay,' Rishaan introduced himself.

'Kiara Sen. My first day in Star.'

Rishaan didn't know whether to thank or curse his stars for these were his last five days in office.

'Wow! Congrats. Which department?'

'Brand Marketing.'

'Oh. I'm in Programming.'

The lift reached the third floor. Kiara had to exit, much to Rishaan's dislike. As she walked away, he couldn't take his eyes off her athletic back, ogling at it for whatever brief moment he could. He wondered if she found time to work out regularly, or if she was naturally blessed with the shapely assets. This wasn't the common girl he'd bump into by the dozen. There was something refreshingly different about her, or so he thought. Attitude it was, perhaps! She was confident, yet fragile. She was damn sexy and seemed equally intelligent. 'An impressively eclectic package!' he ruminated.

As Rishaan went through the chores, he kept thinking about the girl. He quite liked her name—Kiara Sen—short and simple. 'Besides, a Bong woman is anyway quite interesting,' he thought.

The last few days in an organization are those where you push yourself hard to work even as you keep thinking of your life beyond the organization. The dichotomy had Rishaan go out for a stroll twice. As he stepped out he realized that Kiara, being a smoker, might well be out too. This optimism made Rishaan prolong his stay outside to almost half an hour, until the ominous call from his irksome boss made him return. As he waited for the lift to come down, it finally happened. Out walked Kiara. She looked prettier now with her hair left open. Long and lustrous they were! The two exchanged a brief smile with the positions reversed—Rishaan inside the lift and Kiara outside. From the glass wall of the ascending lift, Rishaan kept looking at her until she was out of sight.

After dealing with his boss, Rishaan was still thinking about Kiara. Why did she seem so familiar? He concluded that she was perhaps a cross between Zeenat Aman and Bipasha Basu, two of the sexiest women on the Indian celluloid. But why were the two bumping on each other again and again? He didn't know.

That evening when Rishaan left from office, as he was crossing the street to catch an auto, he saw Kiara waiting on the other side. The hope that they may become auto-mates again had him run across the road, disregarding his own safety. He missed her by a whisker as Kiara got into an auto and sped away.

That evening Rishaan had to struggle quite a bit to bring his stranded car back to action. By the time he had gotten a can of petrol to fill up the empty coffer and managed to start the engine, it was already late evening. He hopped into the car, started the engine and was ready to leave, when a familiar face popped in front. Familiar face in an unfamiliar dress: micro-denim shorts and a sleeveless light-green top. Kiara Sen it was!

'Hey what a pleasant surprise,' she beamed up realizing that it was Rishaan.

'How come you...here..?' Rishaan asked.

'Well, I live here... On the eighth floor of this building,' she informed. 'Do you stay close by?'

'Nope. I had left my car here.'

Fifteen minutes later, Rishaan and Kiara were sitting at the Gloria Jeans Coffee outlet, sipping cappuccino and green tea respectively. He could make out that she was quite an object of desire at the café, which actually made him an object of envy for people around.

Rishaan learnt that Kiara was from Delhi. She had a Bong father and an Assamese mother. She had done her Bachelor's and MBA from Pune, and had been in Mumbai for the last one year. This was her second job. Hence, he calculated her age to be roughly around twenty-four. She seemed a fitness freak and rued that her gym was shut for maintenance.

Kiara learnt that Rishaan was from Lucknow. After having done a course in journalism from Delhi, he came to Mumbai three years ago to pursue a career in scriptwriting and direction. But the need to make ends meet in the city had him first assist a director for a year and then take up a channel job. Now, he had decided to quit his job and pursue a couple of film scripts he had been meaning to work on for a very long time.

'So how old are you?' she asked him.

'I guess I would be a year or two older to you.'

'And how old am I?' she asked. 'Twenty-four?'

'Oh! I just turned twenty-four last week. But how did you know?' she asked surprised.

'Ah! Well, a writer tends to do his own calculations.'

'Oh really? Damn interesting!'

For the first time, he saw her laugh. She looked so beautiful, so genuine, so real.

'You know what, I used to write great stories in school and always thought I'd be a writer,' she revealed.

'Really? And then?'

'Well, life took an unexpected turn. My family went through a difficult phase. And I stopped dreaming.'

Rishaan found it strange that a person whom he'd met for the first time barely twelve hours ago on the street nearby, had begun to open up to him. And though they were engaged in an absorbing conversation, he found it hard to ignore her long, athletic legs.

They took leave soon after.

That night Rishaan kept thinking about this new female whom he had bumped into several times since that morning. She seemed to have a deadly mix of physical attractiveness and substance in her; a mixture that had already resulted in a craving to speak to her again. But he didn't have her number yet. Rishaan wondered how he had forgotten to take her number. He instead decided to check her out on Facebook. There were at least a dozen Kiara Sens. Yeah, there was one who looked like the Kiara he had met. The photograph had Kiara and supposedly her mother on a foreign holiday. Rishaan was tempted to send her a friend request, a temptation he eventually resisted. He did manage to view some of Kiara's albums though. One album from her college days created four years ago had some pictures of hers with a handsome guy which suggested a close bonding. Another recent album created eight months ago showed her on a wild holiday with a group of girlfriends, while yet another had pictures from a trek to Ladakh. Some of the pictures gave away a Bohemian perception, the sort which whets up male fantasy.

Kiara's pictures, her words, the way she looked, her dresses, her smoking a cigarette, all kept playing out in Rishaan's head till very late in the night, keeping slumber at bay. He found it unusual that a day that began with betrayal from Shama ended in hope created by a stranger. Myraid thoughts and images floated in his mind as he did what soothed him best in such situations: Picked up his cellphone, shuffled through it for his favourite romantic playlist and tapped on the first one that appeared.

'What a number! Perfect for the mood.'

An emotional song 'In Dino' from the movie *Life in a... Metro* played out loud in continuum.

Three

> *We don't meet people by accident.*
> *They are meant to cross our path for a reason.*

It is strange that when the craving to meet or talk to someone becomes intense, the person seems that much more elusive. When Rishaan went past Kiara's house in his car the next morning, he was quite hopeful he might see her waiting on the road for an auto. But that was not to be! He even stopped the car by the side of the road and waited for a few minutes mulling over whether he should ask the watchman of the building if Kiara had already left. But he was quick to realize the absurdity of the thought.

A few minutes later, at a traffic signal, in an auto standing alongside his car, he spotted a pair of shapely legs covered with black formal trousers and an elegant pair of heeled office shoes. He turned a bit more to get a better view of her. Kiara Sen it was, fiddling with her BBM. He honked to catch her attention. She reciprocated with a warm smile, realizing that her traffic signal neighbour was the same guy she had been bumping into quite eerily since last morning. But by then, the signal had turned green and Rishaan had to negotiate a safe passage in order to avoid being bombarded once again with invectives from fellow drivers.

Rishaan abandoned speed to be the safe driver he never was, driving closely behind Kiara's auto, hoping they might time their entry together into office and manage to exchange a few words in the lift. They did find themselves in the lift at the same time, but with four other people from the ad-sales team, all engaged in an animated discussion over the revised unrealistic targets set by the boss. So, Rishaan's conversation with Kiara was restricted to the minimal exchange of pleasantries.

That whole day the two did not bump into each other. In fact, at six in the evening, when Rishaan was entering a meeting, he saw her in the glass lift with her bag, leaving for the day. While crossing her building later, the same evening, Rishaan turned around, hoping against hope to see if she could be spotted anywhere around. He wasn't as lucky as the previous evening.

Wednesday was bad. Rishaan had to go to the shoot to hand over certain responsibilities to the new executive producer of the show. The tortuous journey to the sets in Vasai, where the serial was being shot, and back consumed his entire day. He didn't go to office at all. On his way back, he stopped at the coffee shop near Kiara's house, hoping he might catch her. He sat there for an hour sipping a cappuccino, all alone and completely exhausted. And just when he was about to pay the bill and leave, he saw Kiara walk in with two young guys. These guys seemed a bit ultra-cool—one had a pony tail and sported an ear ring, the other was damn good looking but quite pansy.

'Hey, hi Rishaan, how come you're here?' she asked, surprised.

'Well...well... I had a meeting with my show's writer here.'

'Ah I see...' Kiara didn't find Rishaan's reply convincing, but didn't show it either.

She introduced him to the two guys as her friends from Symbiosis College and invited him to join in. Rishaan was tempted to stay back but realizing that he would be giving in too easily, chose otherwise. As he left, he noted her dress: it was the same pair of t-shirt and shorts it was, but with a different colour combination. Even as Rishaan started his car, he kept gazing in through the exterior glass of the café. Kiara sat cross-legged, engrossed in a casual banter with the two men seated on either side. For no obvious reason, Rishaan felt a tinge of jealousy growing inside him which persisted for a good couple of hours. That night, when Rishaan hit the bed he felt lonesome. To his surprise, he had already begun to miss Kiara.

Thursday again they couldn't meet, except for a few seconds on the lift, that too towards the fag end of the day and joined by her colleague, Rhea. And hence, there was little that they could talk beyond the very basic exchange of courtesies. As they got out of the lift, Rishaan surprised himself with an unexpected, impromptu query.

'Hey, can I have your number please?'

Rhea was too preoccupied to react any differently than to give it out rather nonchalantly.

Friday was supposed to be Rishaan's last day in office. The day coincided with Star TV's annual bash for its employees and associated workers, which was to take place in the evening at Bandra's Taj Land's End.

Rishaan just felt too lethargic to stick to schedule on the last day. Moreover, he had to ready an extra pair of party dress which he'd be carrying along so that he could go the party directly instead of coming back home.

He sauntered into the office only by noon, inundated by myriad thoughts and emotions. He was happy that from next day he would no longer be tied up all day carrying other people's agendas. He felt optimistic he could now pursue, full-fledged, the aspirations that had brought him to the city. For a change, Kiara's thoughts were on the backburner.

And then *she* appeared. A vibrant round-neck yellow t-shirt and faded jeans—Friday dressing it was—made her look so much more alluring than she did in her formal wear. Rishaan felt tempted to ask her if they could go for the party together. But held back. He barely knew her to take that liberty. Wouldn't he seem like a pile-on?

On second thoughts, this was his last day in office. How did it matter what she thought? He would most likely not meet her again. And if he indeed wanted to continue meeting her in future, this was the moment to strike. He would have to take a chance, he thought.

Rishaan had started typing a message to Kiara when it dawned on him that an email might help explain his position better. Since all official mail ids at Star followed a fixed pattern, he knew what her id would be. Half an hour later, the mail that went out of Rishaan's mailbox read thus:

Dear Kiara, have you ever experienced that addictively exciting feeling when you want to bump into a stranger more often? I have been feeling it ever since we shared the auto ride five mornings ago. Would you mind if I drive you to the party tonight? ...Rishaan

Hardly had he sent the mail when Mita, his boss with whom he shared a caustic love–hate relationship, tapped him from behind.

'Rishaan, listen I don't have my car today. So I will come with you to the party. Okay?'

Rishaan instantly concocted a story about a friend of his being admitted in hospital and that he'd have to visit the friend before going to the party.

'Useless, you are,' complimented the tomboyish Mita, before going away.

He finally sent the mail and within minutes, received a notification that the mail had been read. But a response eluded him, making him jittery. He spent nearly an hour at the canteen hoping to meet her. She did walk in later, with two of her colleagues, busy discussing something important. The three walked right past him, without even noticing him. Given his anxious state of mind, Rishaan thought she had ignored him on purpose.

It was 5 p.m. and Rishaan had given up hopes of the beautiful stranger accompanying him in his car. He felt bad for his boss and decided to take her along instead.

'Mita, actually my friend's condition has improved a bit. So I can visit him tomorrow and we can travel to the party together,' he went and told Mita.

Rishaan came back to his cubicle and refreshed his computer to check the mails one last time before shutting down, hoping against odds to receive a reply.

'Pop' buzzed the computer; the bottom right of the screen

read '1 new message'. Rishaan glared at the screen, he had received a mail.

He clumsily searched the mouse and clicked on the flashing message. It was from Kiara. She had sent a reply which read:

Dear Rishaan, at times one feels more comfortable chatting with a stranger by choice than with colleagues who are virtually thrust upon you. I had agreed to go with a colleague, but now I think I'd prefer travelling with you. I just went and told that my friend is admitted in the hospital. Looking forward to your company. ...Kiara

Rishaan felt super excited. How uncanny was it that she and him had concocted similar excuses! But what would he tell his boss now?

Five minutes later, he walked into his boss's cabin with a grim visage.

'What happened?' asked she.

'I'm afraid I will have to leave right away.'

A silent pause followed as the boss kept waiting for his next words.

'I just got the news, my friend has passed away.'

♦

At 7 p.m., Rishaan and Kiara reached Kiara's Juhu flat. They stopped for a quick change before heading to Bandra.

The house was quite messed up, as she had no idea she'd be getting a visitor. Clothes were strewn all over the place, some looked recently washed and dried and others just hanging around. Also among the cluster were her undergarments. The latter, couldn't escape Rishaan's notice.

'I'm sorry. I've told my maid so many times to keep them

properly before leaving.' She explained apologetically, folding them away.

'You stay here alone?'

'No, I have a room-mate, Rimi. She is currently out of station on an official trip.'

Kiara lead Rishaan to Rimi's room, while she went to her own and locked the door from inside.

Rishaan changed into a satin grey shirt and tie, with a matching blazer to compliment them. He gelled his usually unkempt longish hair to look more party ready. Rishaan had this unusual ability to look equally good in both formal and casual attires. Moreover, he wasn't conventionally good-looking; his good looks emanated from the customary confidence inherent in his personality.

When Kiara came out after changing, the sight left Rishaan mesmerized. A crimson red backless gown it was, exposing her back enough to whet any man's fantasy. The dress reassured Rishaan that he was truly in company of a classy bombshell. The gown had a set of strings on the back, systematically entangled to each other, and in need of some adjustments. Since Kiara's hand couldn't reach that part of her back, Rishaan had to do the needful. He spent a few seconds simply staring at the pores of her skin and came to a conscious conclusion that he'd be more than happy to do something of this sort every day.

'Thanks Rishaan. Are you ready?' she asked.

Rishaan nodded, distractedly.

'Hey your tie isn't knotted properly,' she observed.

'Yeah, I always get it wrong on the second knot, hence I keep to one,' he explained sheepishly.

'But that doesn't look good. Wait, I'll tie it for you.'

Kiara unknotted his tie and tied it all over again with the confidence of someone who does it every day.

'How do you know this?' asked a surprised Rishaan.

Kiara took a moment to reply.

'Well, my ex-boyfriend used to wear a tie to office every day,' said she, reluctantly.

This information was revealed in a rather matter-of-fact way, leaving Rishaan wondering—should he take the chance and ask her more about her ex-boyfriend? On second thoughts, he felt that it would seem premature. Besides, they were already very late for the party. So he dropped that thought and without delaying any further took off for the party with the lady in red.

For the next forty-five minutes, as Rishaan negotiated through the Friday-evening traffic, Kiara and he got to know a little bit more about each other. Kiara's dad, an army officer, had left the Mom and baby Kiara to marry another woman. Over the years, Kiara had grown very close to her mom, who was a professor of History in the Delhi University. Further more, she had completed her schooling from the prestigious Welhams' Boarding School at Dehradun. And had lived for a year with a family in New Zealand as part of a students' exchange programme. This, Rishaan thought, explained her super confident, independent streak. Rishaan, for his part, had never been abroad. He had lived a simple, rather boring life— his father, a civil engineer with the PWD and mother, a school teacher.

In as much as Rishaan had a fair idea of her relationship status, he was tempted to ask her about it. After thinking a bit on how he should broach it, he finally asked her rather directly.

'Are you seeing someone?'

For a moment, Kiara was taken aback by the directness of the query. But on second thoughts, she reasoned that a guy who helped her dress was within his rights to ask her that.

'No. I recently broke off. We were seeing each other for the last few months.'

'I see.'

'What about you?'

'Well I keep falling for women who love others, while women who fall for me, don't find favour with me.'

'Which means you've never been in a relationship?'

Rishaan was a bit taken in by the bluntness. He couldn't complain though, as it was he who had initiated it. But what Kiara said next left him stunned.

'I hope you are not a virgin.'

He didn't know how to react. She had pricked a raw nerve. His only sexual indulgence was with a girl whom he met at a college fest and then never met again. Shama, on the other hand never allowed it to go beyond kissing and necking. It made her believe she was still within conservative limits.

On seeing Rishaan fluster, Kiara knew what it was. And so, controlling her laughter as best as she could, quickly changed the topic.

Rishaan was quite in awe of his co-passenger's spunk. She didn't seem a stranger anymore.

'Rishaan and Kiara; sounded nice together. Will she be *the* one for me?' Rishaan wondered.

Four

Knowing how to be solitary is central to the art of loving.
When we can be alone, we can be with others
without using them as a means of escape.
—BELL HOOKS

For the next couple of hours, Rishaan and Kiara were in different groups. On the sidelines of the main party, the channel's programming department had organized a small farewell for Rishaan which had a cake-cutting ritual with all his team members. The team also gave Rishaan a combined gift: a high-end Blackberry phone. As soon as the mini-celebration was over, the programming team quickly got their drinks and joined the others at the sprawling sea-facing lawns of the main venue.

Rishaan immediately ran his sight around to figure out where Kiara was. He finally spotted her from her cleavage. With a drink in her hand, she was talking to two very senior executives, both vying hard to grab her attention. Rishaan had a notion that senior executives in their forties were the most 'tharki' of all men. And here he was proved right. With a glass of whisky each in their hands, they tried hard to impress the pretty woman in front chatting about their fitness regimen, love for travel and theatre et al, unaffected by her expressions of ennui.

As Rishaan looked around, he realized there was only one other woman who was dressed as seductively as Kiara. He wondered if Kiara was an attention seeker or just too liberated to care for others. He remembered their conversation in the car—her confiding about her parents' divorce. Would it have resulted in her being the bohemian that she seemed to be? He remembered her referring to her ex-boyfriend. The fact that she tied his tie often meant they perhaps lived-in together. And then she also mentioned that the relationship lasted only a few months. She must be quite fast then, no? Was she a flirt? Was she into men? Did she value relationships?

Rishaan wondered what was making him dig so deep into the mind of the stranger, who was suddenly beginning to feel less so. As two other men gathered around Kiara, Rishaan realized that she would remain the cynosure of the party and his chances of spending quality time with her were bleak. Instead he turned his attention to his colleagues and friends, whom he would not be able to meet so frequently henceforth.

Rishaan was chatting with two people when much to his surprise, he saw Kiara come and stand near him. She smiled at him and looked slightly inebriated. Rishaan was quick to turn his attention to her.

'So, how many pegs down are you?' he asked her.

'This is the fourth, I guess.'

'Wow! You've got some appetite...'

'What about you?'

'This is my second drink.'

Rishaan wondered if Kiara was seeking some sort of escape in intoxication, or if she habitually enjoyed going overboard. They walked away from the crowd to that stretch of the garden that was closest to the sea. It was a full moon night and the breeze was as good as it could ever be in Mumbai.

'You must be feeling cold. Should I give you my blazer?' Rishaan offered, nearly taking it off.

'Actually, I'm loving it. Isn't this the closest that you can get to winter here?'

For the next few moments, Rishaan and Kiara stood there soaking in the majestic ambience. The strong breeze blowing across seemed pregnant with intuitive hopes of a new alignment.

'Do you mind stepping out for a walk? I feel like going closer to the sea,' said Kiara, spiritedly.

Rishaan, for his part, didn't mind a lady calling the shots. They stepped out for a private walk, not bothered about what others in the party might think. At eleven in the night, Bandstand still looked a busy place. Mumbai's latest tourist hub, Shahrukh Khan's bungalow, Mannat, was surrounded by a good number of starry-eyed fans waiting outside, hoping to catch a glimpse of the elusive star. There were families out on the streets for a post-dinner drive. And then there were the dating couples, some of whom looked pretty much like strangers getting to know each other, while most others seemed madly in love (or lust).

As Rishaan and Kiara walked on the promenade, they couldn't help wondering to which category did they belong. The breeze blew across them, making their hair fly. Rishaan was tempted to hold her hand and so he did, to which Kiara reacted with a momentary surprise. Rishaan sensed she didn't like it and pulled his hand away. A few moments later though, Kiara stretched her hand for his and held it more robustly. They walked past other couples, hand in hand, wondering if Bandstand would have them visit her more often in future.

Kiara, restless as she mostly was, soon felt an urge to go into the water.

'Hey, Rishaan, follow me,' she said impulsively and rushed towards the rock stones, closer to the sea.

'Kiara, wait...there could be snakes or insects...,' cautioned Rishaan, quickly following behind her

Kiara didn't care. Exuding child-like excitement, she treaded towards the sea, until she realized that she wouldn't be able to go further with her heels on. So, holding her sandal in one hand and balancing herself with the other, she stood atop a rock stone and called out for Rishaan.

'Rishaan come here...this is such a lovely place to be...,' she beamed.

Just then Rishaan's phone rang. It was a call from his parents. Since Rishaan was unable to take their previous calls, he decided to answer it, lest they call again in another inopportune moment. Left to herself for some time, Kiara settled on the rock stone, edging the sea. Two drunk men, who were hovering around, thought she was alone and made a pass at her. One whistled at her calling her, '*O meri hot hot chocolate brownie.*' The other went a step ahead and made an offer. 'What do you charge for a night?' asked he, exuding suicidal confidence.

'Sorry?' said a baffled Kiara.

'Come over...we'll make you rich,' he went on to say.

By the time Rishaan ended the call and turned around to join her, he saw something really bizarre happening. Kiara walked towards the men, who were gleefully whistling aloud, thinking she'd consented. As she reached closer, Kiara suddenly took her sandal and hit the nastier man hard on his face with the heels. The man, already heavily drunk, was shaken by the impact and fell off the rock. As soon as the other man, a baldie, started to help him out. Kiara hit him twice two hard blows on his head. The baldie shrieked in pain.

Kiara unleashed some of her choicest invectives on them, challenging them if they were still interested in knowing her rates for the night. The two men, now in much pain, made a hasty exit.

Kiara turned back to see Rishaan standing right behind her. Rishaan was dazed by what he had seen and it showed in his expression.

'Wow! You managed to shoo them away?'

'I'd have killed them tonight if they had touched me,' she said rather coolly, making Rishaan think for a second if she had done that before.

'By the way, have you ever saved a woman from being molested?' she turned and asked him, surprising him with the sudden query.

Rishaan shook his head.

'Exactly! You wouldn't have done that today either if those men would have molested me. It's high time we women change our attitudes. We need to be self-equipped to deal with such demons instead of depending on men.'

Well, she certainly was high and perhaps even had a weird sense of humour, but what Rishaan couldn't figure out was whether he was actually being reprimanded for leaving her alone on the isolated rock stone.

'Listen, Kiara I'm sorry...Mom had called me thrice since evening and I...'

Kiara was on her own trip and barely heard what he said. Instead, she went back to the rock stone on the edge, her sandal still in her hands. Standing atop the rock stone, she started mumbling to herself.

'Chemical castration! That's the word. Such pests should be chemically castrated. Another way to end crimes against women is judo training. It's simple. I have had a bit of training when I was in class VIII.' She began to demonstrate her skills at judo, making Rishaan very jittery; one wrong step and she would fall in the water. Hence, Rishaan quickly opened his shoes, folded up his trousers and rushed closer to Kiara.

Kiara, by now, seemed to have lost it completely.

'My lord, I demand death penalty for all rapists and life imprisonment for all eve-teasers, and I shall be on an indefinite hunger strike until my demands are met,' she roared, with little sense of who she was addressing. And then she slipped! Rishaan had been waiting for the eventuality like a fielder in the deep waiting for the batsman to mistime a big hit. Kiara, who had shut her eyes, fearing the worst, fell straight into Rishaan's arms. She opened her eyes and looked in utter disbelief. Rishaan held on to her in that position realizing that it was a once-in-a-lifetime moment. Neither was Kiara in any sort of hurry. They looked into each other's eyes, and even perhaps hoped they could get a bit more romantic and later blame it on the alcohol.

Sadly, the magical moment was disturbed by an intrusive

voice calling from behind.

'Eeh. Kai karto?'

They turned to see an obese police constable, who looked livid and outraged by their indiscretion.

'Come out. Stop this indecent behaviour. I'll make you spend the night in the lock-up,' he threatened.

Still holding her in his arms, while she possessively held on to her sandal, Rishaan carried her out. As they reached close to where the constable stood, Rishaan gently put her down.

It took a tedious round of negotiations to convince the constable not to take them to the police station. The constable had himself preferred the other option.

'Give me five hundred rupees if you want to sort it here,' he demanded brazenly.

The demand took Kiara on another trip.

'Five hundred rupees for what? For holding me in his arms and saving my life?' she roared.

Rishaan tried to calm her down and quickly took out his wallet to end the madness as soon as possible. But Kiara chose to do things her own way.

'Fair enough! You want money, right?'

She turned towards Rishaan and planted a kiss each on both his cheeks.

'He deserved this reward for this bravery,' she told the constable. She then grabbed Rishaan's wallet and took out a thousand rupee note.

'Here, take it, you greedy fool, five hundred for me falling in his arms and another five hundred for what I did just now.'

Hardly had the confused constable held the note than Rishaan, influenced by Kiara's madness, clicked a picture of the constable taking the bribe. Kiara was amused by the picture.

'Now give back the money and just get lost before we take you to the police station for accepting a bribe,' she warned the constable.

The constable retreated looking amazed by the lady's antics. Rishaan looked as flummoxed. Super excited, Kiara jumped for a high five. Till now Rishaan had thought she was refreshingly different. Now he was beginning to get an idea of just how crazy she could be.

'What happened?' she asked. 'You look dazed.'

'N...no...thing.'

Kiara held Rishaan's hand and started walking over the promenade again. As they strolled along, Kiara enquired about Rishaan's personal life.

'So what keeps a *seedha-saadha* good-looking dude like you single?' She asked him rather inquisitively.

Rishaan wasn't sure if he wanted to talk about it all over again. But when Kiara put forth the query, in the fragile state of mind that he was, he felt inclined to pour his heart out. He spoke about his unrequited love, and why love in his life never quite seemed to become a two-way traffic.

'You know what, good guys are increasingly scarce nowadays. So don't worry, a hot, sexy and intelligent girl is going to find you out soon,' reassured Kiara.

'Oh really. Thanks for the optimism.'

A moment of ruminative calm intervened; both of them perhaps wondered why love so often needs to be unrequited. And then, Kiara broke the silence by asking if they should return to the party.

'Yes, of course,' said Rishaan, realizing he'd had little choice in the decision-making, all evening.

As they walked back to the Taj Land's End, they crossed a Toyota Fortuner that was parked by the roadside. The front door opened, almost hitting Kiara, and out came a handsome-looking, seemingly-sophisticated-tall man in his mid-forties. He almost looked like the very suave character actor, Rajat Kapoor.

For a moment, both Kiara and the man were shocked to see each other. Kiara soon gathered herself and holding Rishaan's hand walked ahead. The man kept looking at Kiara until a blonde babe sitting on the co-passenger's seat called him. Rishaan found this a bit strange.

'Did you know him?' he asked Kiara.

Kiara didn't answer, though her visage bore a certain mark of anger. Before Rishaan could say anything more, they had reached the party venue. Soon, they split into their respective groups again, Kiara gulping down a couple of pegs more, while Rishaan too exceeded his normal quota with a 'neat' peg of vodka.

Rishaan was growing a bit restless. There was something unusual that this babe had done to him. He was lost thinking what a truly thrilling day it had been: the funny, formal exchange of mails between them; that tempting moment when he helped her adjust her dress, enjoying the most uncensored view of her seductive bare back; them walking down the breezy promenade amidst some really romantic couples; and finally the double adventure involving first the eve-teasers and then the avaricious constable. What bothered him a wee bit was the suave gentleman in his late forties looking at Kiara in a somewhat strange way and the normally outspoken Kiara evading a reply.

Rishaan's boss, Mita, a heavy drinker herself, had been watching Rishaan grapple with his thoughts alone, until Rishaan saw her looking at him and responded with a sheepish smile.

'Aaj ki hogaya tainu?' she asked him in Punjabi, a language she employed more freely after getting drunk. 'You made your friend die and instead of mourning for him you landed up at the party looking like a lost Romeo.'

Rishaan struggled for an answer, even as the chaos in his head had become too obvious to hide. He looked across at the other side of the venue. Kiara was surrounded by two new potential suitors—one, Rishaan's junior from the programming team and the other, a marketing guy. Also with them was a studious looking, plain jane who was trying hard not to be left out of the conversation. Rishaan noticed that a peculiar music was being played; alternating between the best retro songs of English and Hindi.

Mita smiled at Rishaan, making him more conscious. She then held out a neat drink that she was carrying, and with a mischievous glint in her eyes, gestured him to gulp it down.

Rishaan gulped it down at once. Two full pegs and two neats down, he felt audacious like never before, particularly given that the song playing on the system, only prodded his spirit. He zestfully started walking towards Kiara on an impulse. Kiara was still surrounded by people when she heard a familiar voice call her name. She turned to see Rishaan standing right next to her. He had an impassioned look on his face, which was rightly indicative of him having consumed more liquor than he could handle.

Rishaan came close to her, held her hand and took her away to a small open space right at the centre of the venue.

With the song seeming just apt to convey his feelings at that point, he held her closely and broke into a ball dance. The move surprised Kiara, though she felt quite flattered to co-operate. For the next couple of minutes, they matched steps to Chris De Burgh's classic, 'Lady in Red', that also doubled as Rishaan's unspoken dedication.

As Rishaan and Kiara danced, absorbed completely in the lyrics and in each other's moves, they did not realize that a crowd of no less than fifty people had gathered around them, mesmerized by their natural chemistry... And the song went on...

It took the couple some claps and a bunch load of whistles from a few over enthusiastic guests to bring them out of their reverie. And as they looked around, people seemed either genuinely happy for them or outright jealous. The isolation got them even closer and made them seek comfort in each other.

Five

> *Between what is said and not meant and
> what is meant and not said, most of love is lost.*
> —KHALIL GIBRAN

At 2.10 a.m. when most of Mumbai would have dozed off, Rishaan and Kiara sat on a luxurious sofa in the sea-facing poolside cafe of Novotel, Juhu. They sat on the two ends of the sofa with a small space between them, Rishaan's palm clasping Kiara's. Lost in thought, they looked towards the dark sea, with nothing much visible except a few illuminated dots in the firmament, perhaps an indication of the returning fishing boats.

Rishaan and Kiara had left the party early and a bit abruptly, not bothering about public perceptions. They now felt so comfortable in each other's company that others didn't matter. They wanted more and more of each other and exclusively so. Hence, while on their way back, Rishaan drove the car straight into what was his favourite spot in Mumbai—another sea-front, an even better one. Rishaan and Kiara had been sitting there for past half an hour, sipping black coffee in a bid to undo the effects of liquor.

The breeze was same as before. What was different was a new found equanimity or stillness between them. Now, they didn't necessarily require words to keep the communication alive. A mere exchange of look or holding of hands sufficed; and the fact that they had reached this stage so soon carried a sense perhaps of things to come.

Suddenly, Kiara got up and moved towards the edge of the cafe, which seemed like a large open balcony. Beneath it was the sand of the Juhu beach and 50 metres away, the sea. Kiara bent forward and rested herself on the waist-high wall of the hotel, gazing straight into the sea. Rishaan followed her inquisitively and stood right behind her. Kiara was absorbed in her thoughts and had not noticed Rishaan come to her. Rishaan felt increasingly sure that Kiara, apart from battling acute forlornness, was perhaps going through a major crisis in her life. It took Kiara sometime to realize that Rishaan was standing right next to her, to which she responded with a sheepish, tentative smile. Rishaan put his hand on her shoulder in a gesture of support. He got a sense that Kiara wanted to open up about something. He felt odd though to question directly. Then, coincidentally, an old song from the Hindi movie *Arth*, 'Tum Itna Jo Muskura Rahe Ho', played out loud on a passer-by's cellphone on the beach below, actually did the job for him.

As the song went on, Rishaan held her with greater authority and had her turn to face him. Looking straight into her eyes, his heart sang aloud. Kiara could feel her defence crumbling.

'I have just come out of a chaotic relationship,' she said, beginning to open up. 'It was the sort of relationship that makes you feel used, abused and cheated. It made me hate myself.'

Kiara was in a relationship with a married man more than two decades older to her. He was her boss in her previous organization.

'It started as a mentor–protégé bonding. It was my first job and when my other batchmates were going through a tough time learning the ropes of the professional world, I was extremely lucky to have such a sweet, caring and supportive mentor. He'd give me amazing freedom to take independent decisions and deal with cases my way, while always being there to guide me. I think that sort of a boss instils huge confidence in you. You grow very fast.'

Rishaan was beginning to squirm at the prospect of discovering unpleasant information that might change his opinion about Kiara completely.

'And then?' he queried, putting up a brave façade.

'The flip side of this sort of mentoring is that it makes you feel ingratiated towards the boss. As we started spending more time together, he began opening up about his personal life. Soon I discovered that he was in a loveless marriage; or so he liked the world to believe. "I've not had sex with my wife since I don't know when... I don't even know about her friends or what she does all day," he would tell me in a way that I later realized was manoeuvred to evoke sympathy. "Marriage is an outdated institution. Don't get married until you've been in a relationship for at least three to four years," he would advise me like a teacher and I'd listen obediently like an awestruck pupil. He was candid about the two affairs he had had outside marriage. When I asked him why he didn't divorce his wife, he told me, "Divorce is not an option when you have two growing-up children at home." It's strange that instead of correcting him for the aberrant life he led, I had started to feel for him. He had supported me so much on the professional front. I guess I tended to reciprocate by trying to bring in some joy in his personal life.'

'Did you sleep with him?' Rishaan asked her rather curtly, though a certain disapproval was apparent in his tenor. It surprised Kiara, but unsure of how to react, she chose to ignore it.

'I would say I fell in love and we made love,' she replied candidly.

'Smart women! They all do it for professional gains and then call it love.' This was the instant thought in Rishaan's head when he heard Kiara's justification. Kiara, on the other hand, seemed to have found an outlet for her pent-up feelings.

'He is probably the smoothest talker I have ever met. It started with him asking me out for dinners when I worked in office till late. These dinners would extend to long philosophical conversations over life. We'd end up discussing just about any and everything under the sun. For me, these conversations gave me a different perspective about looking at things. It enhanced my worldview. Our age difference was such that I valued his experienced insights on most topics.'

Just then a strong gush of breeze blew past them. Kiara shut her eyes for a moment, but Rishaan continued to look at her intently, hoping to discover her full self in the next few minutes.

'Go on.' he said.

'What makes you so curious?'

'The fact that I have developed an interest in you.'

'Really?' she laughed. 'Interest is okay, but let me warn you, I am not the right sort of girl for anything beyond a passing interest. Men who have known me closely, would vouch for that.'

'How many men have you been in a relationship with?'

'Just two.' Rishaan heaved a sigh of relief. He could not get why strange emotions like jealousy and possessiveness were taking control of him. That he was suddenly feeling for this girl. On his prodding, Kiara went on to complete her story.

'You know what, in every complicated relationship that a discerning individual sometimes finds herself entrapped, there are various warning signals that tell you to move out before it's too late. And it happened with me too. We had reached a stage where he wanted to over-share stuff with me. For instance, there were nights when we'd end up chatting online till almost 4 a.m.; then he'd message me in the morning asking which colour shirt he should wear. He'd ask personal stuff like my period cycle. When this started happening, I didn't approve of the proximity that was being imposed upon me. And so, one day, I had a candid talk with him. I told him, "Sir, I really admire you and will always remain grateful to you, but you are a married man, why do you behave with me in a way that is appropriate only with your spouse?" His answer shocked me. He confessed he'd fallen in love with me and that he felt a natural intimacy towards me. He also apologized for it and promised to be more discreet in what he spoke henceforth. For the next few days, he retreated completely and our conversations became as formal and restricted as they were in the first few weeks of knowing each other.'

'Then...?'

'I was an emotional fool. I thought I had hurt him and felt really bad to see him that lonely. I enquired if things were any better on his personal front. I guess he was waiting for this opportunity. That was a busy day in office and he asked if we could meet over dinner. Over dinner, he repeated he loved me and did so without any expectations. That night, when he dropped me home, I felt like a different person. I really fell for his smooth talks and didn't want him to go back to being tortured at home. I asked if he'd like to stay over at my place. He stayed back. In those days, I was staying alone in a studio apartment in Bandra. We slept on the same bed; I made sure that the two pillows I used were placed right between us.'

'You mean nothing happened between the two of you?'

'You think I am a slut?'

'Of course not...then?'

'Four days later, at 3 a.m. when I was fast asleep, my doorbell rang. To my shock, it was him. His face bore a couple of bruises. He told me very reluctantly that his wife and he had had a violent fight and that he had walked out of the house. I let him stay for a few days until he got an alternate accommodation. Those few days changed my life. I realized that I had begun to care for him. In as much as he wanted to extend staying at my place, I realized I wasn't really inclined to have him out either. We were soon in a relationship; one that was as complicated and fucked up as it could be.'

'What went wrong?'

'Everything. I mean the whole idea and experience of being the other woman.'

'But you knew about it right from the start.'

'Of course and that's what surprises me. How could I give in to such a relationship? He was simply playing mind games with me. First he told me that his mother was a cancer patient and would die soon. And until she is alive, he cannot shock her with the news of his divorce and remarriage. When I discovered that his mother had been cured of cancer long ago, he pleaded with me to wait for a year as his son would be giving his Class X exam and he did not want things to go wrong at that front because of him.'

Rishaan could not imagine that someone like Kiara, who appeared so confident and independent, could have a past this complicated.

'Did you love him?' he asked, still trying to understand her.

'For some time I really did. If I didn't I'd be crazy to be in such a relationship. I loved him till I began to realize that he was an incredibly amazing actor. Apart from the stories which he concocted to delay formalizing our relationship, I had started to feel that I was a conquest for him. And that when he had experienced me enough and I began insisting that he clarify our "relationship status", he quickly got himself another rental flat and also started spending more nights at his house. I knew something was amiss. And soon the ugly truth was exposed. One evening he left the office at around 7 for a meeting with a Delhi-based client, who was in town. The meeting was to be followed by dinner. So I knew he would not be in office for at least three to four hours. I walked into his cabin, only to discover that he had left his laptop behind. In another situation, I would have never trespassed into his personal belongings. But here, somehow, I couldn't stop myself from checking his stuff. Thankfully, his email wasn't logged out and since I knew he had a penchant for chatting, I scanned all his chats. After two hours of intensive scanning, what I discovered left me completely shattered. In the last two years, he had probably had affairs with three other women, all much younger to him. At least the chats seemed to corroborate this; with two of the women, he had discussed about his sexual experiences with them and how he wanted to explore newer stuff. Sadly, some of these chats took place in the last few months when he had been promising the moon to me.'

'Hmm... That is disgusting.'

'He walked into the office at around 10.30 p.m. to pick up his laptop. And found me on his seat weeping. He asked me what the matter was. I got up and slapped him hard. I repeated the slap on the other side, striking him even harder. 'Bloody bastard,' I called him and walked away. The next morning, I tendered my resignation. I had to serve a notice period of a month, which got over last Friday.'

Rishaan had heard such scandalous stories of deception but to hear it from a girl who'd lived it first-hand made his blood boil with anger.

'Who the hell is this swine?' he finally asked her.

'Rahul Grover, the guy who got out of the SUV and bumped into me while we were returning to the party.'

Rishaan took a deep breath and reconciled with the thought that the girl he had spent the last few hours, had seen much more of the real world than he had.

◆

As Rishaan drove Kiara back to her apartment, a 5-minute drive from the hotel, he suddenly felt a strong gush of attraction towards her. He hated the thought that these were his last few minutes with her until he didn't know when. He wanted to savour her more. Hence, like a child who drinks his soft-drink slowly when he is finishing off the bottle, he drove the car real slow.

'Safe driving, you see,' he smiled at Kiara as she looked at him surprised. Kiara seemed tentative throughout this last leg of the journey, unsure whether she wanted it to end.

'I will miss this evening,' said Rishaan, as he stopped the car outside her gate.

Kiara got off. She was about to wave a goodbye at him when something stopped her from doing so.

'Care to have a coffee at my place before you finally leave?'

At 3.45 a.m., while Kiara was heating the milk, Rishaan held her from behind and gently slid his hands into hers. It was the sort of soft, comforting, romantic touch that any woman would have found difficult to resist. What followed was a bit unexpected: a kiss deep down her back on the lowest exposed stretch. Kiara shut her eyes enjoying the mystical sensuousness of the moment. He then turned her towards him and planted a couple of gentle pecks on her forehead and the eyebrows. What followed was a sudden passionate smooch for which Kiara wasn't prepared. Nonetheless, she didn't resist it, surprising herself to no end. Only after Rishaan was done, did she gently push him back.

'Have your coffee and go,' she said in an obfuscated tone that brought out the struggle between her head and her heart. One part of her wanted to give in to this guy with whom her chemistry seemed so natural; the other exhorted her not to trust someone so soon, especially after her previous betrayal.

Rishaan was consumed with intense infatuation; he had never experienced something like this before. He moved towards her once again meaning to embrace her and held her face with his hands rather passionately, kissing her again until Kiara pushed him back rather agitatedly.

'Stop it, Rishaan. Just because you've seen my weak side doesn't mean you can take advantage,' she snubbed him.

'I...I...I wasn't taking any advantage,' Rishaan's words faltered, partly due to the fear that he might have indeed crossed the line and partly due to the impact of Kiara's snub.

For a minute, both Rishaan and Kiara found themselves in a very awkward situation. Kiara, in as much as she was holding herself back, was also feeling a strong natural attraction towards this guy. Through the course of the evening, they had ceased to be strangers. Even after hours of heart-to-heart chats, they didn't quite seem to have had enough of each other. They thirsted for more. Had Rishaan's physical indiscretion not hampered the natural flow of things, they'd perhaps still be talking their hearts out like they had done in the last few hours.

'I should leave now. Goodnight,' said Rishaan, breaking the uneasy, quiet spell.

Kiara, by now, was being pulled apart by two very strong divergent forces. One wanted her to be left alone. The other wanted her to have this guy by her side forever. As she coped with the tussle, Rishaan quietly opened the door. He stepped out and waited for the lift to come up. Kiara followed him to the door, feeling increasingly restless seeing him leave in this rather abrupt way. The lift arrived and the doors opened.

Rishaan looked at her, bid her a sedate goodbye and stepped inside the lift. At this point, something happened to Kiara. On an impulse, she ran into the lift and kissed Rishaan longingly. For a moment Rishaan was taken aback, until he too got the drift and reciprocated just as passionately. By the time the lift reached the ground floor from her fifth floor apartment, Rishaan and Kiara found themselves engaged in a wild lip-lock. Rishaan quickly pressed the fifth-floor button, ensuring that the indulgence continued unaffected and got back to serving her lips and beyond, first her neck and then even below. He pressed the lift button twice over, ensuring that the duration of their lip-lock surpassed the longest one in movies by a neat margin.

A few minutes later, Kiara and Rishaan were in Kiara's bedroom. The intense oral activity had laid the foundation for its carnal extension. Kiara unbuttoned Rishaan's shirt, getting full-view of his unshaven torso. She liked it that way and quite despised men who aped womanly ways of getting rid of body hair. She gently caressed his chest, While Rishaan playfully pulled off her gown. The view of her bare bosom left him virtually zonked. He wondered if all that was unfolding in front of him was for real or just an extended voyeuristic trip of his.

Rishaan gently rubbed his tongue against her nipple. Kiara felt a peculiar sensation that had her aroused instantly and like never before. Less than 5 minutes later, Rishaan entered her, unable to hold back the orgasm. After a brief gap, Rishaan and Kiara couldn't help themselves from getting into the act again. This time though, the act was more gentle and entailed prolonged foreplay. Rishaan started by kissing her shapely thighs and then caressing her legs with the sensuous softness of a deft masseur. Kiara licked his ears producing another peculiar sensation of libidinous ecstasy. They felt and discovered each other exhaustively until they made out a second time.

By 5.30 a.m., around the time the very first sounds of the birds' crooning became audible, Kiara was fast asleep. Rishaan, on the other hand, lay by her side, staring blankly at the rotating fan. This was an unprecedented experience for him. Had it been another girl, given his subconscious chauvinist mooring, he would have probably been dismissive of her character. Plus, he still harboured doubts about Kiara. But the equally strong, propelling attraction that he felt towards her, arrested his doubting proclivities. And yet a few moments later, the doubts would resurface more menacingly.

He resolved to confront his doubts head-on. And so, after much thought, he probably had a semblance of an answer: the girl he had romanced with all night and eventually made love to was until a week ago somebody else's 'other woman'. He hated this realization. A counterthought even had him try and give the benefit of doubt to her. What if she had genuinely fallen in love with her ex-boss and indeed hoped to marry him in future? Would he still consider her Grover's 'other woman'? With more thought at work, he concluded that that this still wouldn't give her immunity from being called the other woman in a married man's life.

At 7 in the morning, jaded and thirsting for sleep, Rishaan quietly got up and left Kiara's house. Just before leaving, he turned back to have one last view of her. In sleep, she looked as innocent as he would have wanted her to be.

Instead of driving home, Rishaan drove ahead to the Versova beach, where he sipped a cup of tea at the roadside stall and watched the first rays of the gleaming golden-sun settle on the clear blue-sea. He wondered if the transition in the colour of the water glimmering on the surface of the sea was anyway indicative of the transformation that was taking place in his life.

Unable to sort out these conundrums, he drove back home, crashed on bed and pressed himself to sleep.

Six

> *When love is not madness it is not love.*
> —PEDRO CALDERÓN DE LA BARCA

When Rishaan woke up it was already noon. He stretched over a searching hand for his cell phone and was surprised to find five missed calls from Kiara. His thoughts about the previous night had him laze around in bed for another hour. During this time, he got two more calls from Kiara, but chose not to answer. He wasn't sure if Kiara would want to talk about what happened last night. He wasn't sure about what he would say if she did initiate.

It was only after Rishaan had his bath and lunch that he felt he was in the right frame of mind to call her back. And so he did. And he called her thrice after that and twice in the evening. But the calls remained unanswered, leaving him restless yet again.

Kiara, at her end, spent her day battling her own quandaries. Was she really prepared for a new relationship at this stage? Or was the physical indulgence between her and Rishaan just a momentary act of indiscretion which she must forget? Was it so frivolous that it could be forgotten so easily?

When her calls to Rishaan went unanswered, she grew very anxious and called up her best friend, Diya. After a lengthy chat with Diya, who actually gave her a dressing down of sorts, Kiara felt quite depressed. To divert her mind, she immersed herself in reading up some heavy official documents she had to work on for next week. By the time Rishaan called her back, she had consciously cut herself off from thinking about what had happened the night before, and was trying hard to control her thoughts from swaying again. For some strange reason she anyway had this notion that Rishaan might not want to meet her again.

As for Rishaan, he had begun to feel quite restless by late evening. He was craving to be with Kiara and relive the mystical experience of the night before. But since Kiara had not answered to his calls, it made him feel guilty about the whole experience. After all, he had initiated the physical indulgence. Had he taken undue advantage of Kiara's fragile emotional state? He tried hard to rubbish these thoughts and kept coaxing himself to believe that Kiara wanted and enjoyed the experience as much as he did. But how could he know her mind for sure?

This mutual confusion inhibited them from messaging each other either.

That night both Kiara and Rishaan found it difficult to sleep. Kiara finally fell asleep around 4.30 in the morning.

The doorbell rang sharp at 9 a.m. When she didn't answer it the first time, it ran rang incessantly, forcing her to abandon sleep and leave bed.

'What the hell? This kachdawala will not even let me sleep on a Sunday morning,' she rued.

In her sleepy state, Kiara picked up her dustbin, opened the door and was about to hurl the garbage at the imagined bin of the scavenger when she suddenly realized the kachdawala looked very different. No it wasn't him. It was Rishaan, carrying two large packets that had breakfast packed from the JW Marriot. She dropped the dustbin and hugged him tight. Taken aback, Rishaan wished she had at least washed her hands.

'I missed you,' she said, holding his face and looking into his eyes. Kiara's sudden bear hug in her sleeveless top and skimpy pair of shorts made the whole situation quite irresistible, giving Rishaan cold feet.

'I...I...I messed you. Sorry, I missed you too,' he responded nervously. Rishaan had got a special continental breakfast packed for her, hoping that would help him woo her back; and here he realized he had actually wasted ₹1,200 which he could have otherwise used more judiciously in his struggles as a freelancer!

As Kiara brushed her teeth, Rishaan laid out the breakfast with the finesse of a waiter working in a 5-star hotel.

'Why didn't you pick up my call yesterday?' Rishaan asked her.

'Why did you go off so abruptly yesterday?' Kiara counter-questioned him.

Both didn't have an answer to many things that were suddenly looking so different and hence settled for a quiet breakfast. Sandwiches, croissants and a pastry each, followed by a glass of canned juice.

'Gosh! This was some breakfast. Thank you!' exclaimed Kiara in sheer delight.

Rishaan responded with a smile. With a mischievous glint in his eyes, it was apparent that his mind wasn't idle. He got up and gestured her to stand. She did so with a curious smile. He lifted her up and made her sit on the table. Then he brought his face close to hers, so close that they could feel each other breathe. As he looked into her eyes, the inevitable happened yet again. Rishaan kissed her hard. As they probed each other's oral contours, an aroused Kiara clasped Rishaan tight with her legs around his waist. Rishaan lifted her up and on an impulse took her straight into the bath. For the next half an hour, they rinsed each other under the shower and made out, the wet passion making the experience far more ethereal than the one before.

Rishaan and Kiara spent the rest of Sunday in the house like a live-in couple if not a married one, doing sweet nothings. While Rishaan watched a cricket match between India and Sri Lanka, Kiara got back to studying some office documents.

'You seem very ambitious about your professional goals?' Rishaan asked in passing.

'You bet I am. Not just about my profession, it's actually about everything. I want to give every damn thing in this world my very best. You know why? Because I don't believe there's anything called second best.'

'Hmm...right!'

Kiara added that she had no plans of being in a serious relationship or contemplating marriage at least for the next five years. This bit left Rishaan flummoxed.

'So what's your understanding about the stuff happening between us?' he queried.

'I have no clue,' she said after some thought.

Rishaan felt fairly sure that given the traumatic experience in her last relationship, she purposely wanted to be in denial. He didn't probe any further. For most of the afternoon, Rishaan and Kiara did their own stuff. Kiara smoked some half a dozen cigarettes that day, making Rishaan really uncomfortable.

He was anyway feeling a bit restless. He wanted some sort of reassurance that his sexual indulgence with Kiara was not a mere rebound for her, and that she felt a natural craving for him as much as he had begun to feel for her. 'Oh how naturally women fake,' he thought and tried hard to engage himself in the cricket match that now seemed increasingly lacklustre.

In the evening, Kiara and Rishaan went on a long drive. They spoke about movies. They spoke about sports. They even spoke about Rahul Gandhi, Narendra Modi and the Indian politics. They spoke about everything under the sun, but consciously avoided talking about what was transpiring between them.

Verbalizing a relationship that can't be defined often kills its essence. Rishaan and Kiara were not sure if defining their relationship had become so crucial yet. What both felt sure about was that they wanted to savour the feeling; it was priceless and they did not want to let go of it.

They spent half an hour walking casually on the Marive Drive, holding hands in a reassuring sort of way. Post that they dined at the famous Leopold Café in Colaba, where Kiara avoided a drink to make sure she did not leave any scope for getting carried away once again. By 11 p.m., Rishaan dropped Kiara home and stayed over for the night. There was no explanation needed. All seemed perfectly natural and at peace. That night the two enjoyed a sound sleep, something they had been craving for the past three days.

The next morning, at 8, Kiara left for work, aware of the workload she had to deal with in office. Rishaan chose to extend his slumber finding Kiara's mattress extremely comforting.

A couple of hours later, the doorbell rang. Rishaan was taking a bath, and since he wasn't sure about who it would be, he chose to ignore it. The doorbell started to ring non-stop after that, forcing him to respond without further delay. Soaked in soap lather, with a towel wrapped around his waist, Rishaan opened the door. In front of him was a well-dressed, young lady, with a gigantic suitcase perked beside her, whom he did not recognize. She turned out to be Kiara's flatmate, Rimi. Rimi shrieked in disbelief thinking he was a thief who had sneaked into the house. Rishaan, also clueless as to who she was, pleaded with her to calm down. He kept telling her he was Kiara's friend, but she kept dismissing his claim, saying she knew them all.

Finally, Rimi called up Kiara, even as Rishaan waited wet and bare for things to be sorted out. She locked herself inside her room and returned in some considerable time with a smirk on her face and hand stretched out for an introduction. Kind courtesies done, Rimi left to take a bath in the solitary bath-cum-washroom that left Rishaan with no option but to complete his bath back home.

◆

As Rishaan started a new phase of his life as a freelancer, his lifestyle and habits showed some marked changes. First and foremost, he had to inculcate the discipline to be his own boss and schedule his agenda for the day, week and month, if not beyond that. Apart from focusing on the film script that he had been working on, he also had to chart out a networking schedule for himself and try and meet up A-grade filmmakers. He realized that he needed to identify other exciting subjects to work on in order to multiply his options. More importantly, since revenues weren't going to flow in immediately, he needed to manage his money better. Hence, for the first time, Rishaan became conscious of the mileage his five-year-old Honda City was giving and whether eating out could be avoided at times.

On one hand, Rishaan quite relished the freedom that being out of a job gave him. He no longer had to worry about taking calls from his boss at unwanted hours. And on the other, he was coming to terms with reality on how lonely life could be at times without the company of colleagues and the protection of a parent organization, especially when one is scouting for work. The anxiety had started taking a toll on his mood more frequently than before; it even showed up when he met Kiara over dinners.

Kiara, for her part, had immersed herself in office work. With Star readying for the launch of a new channel in the next few months and with just four people in her team, the workload of creating the brand strategy for the new channel was humongous. Besides, Kiara had begun to find work rather therapeutic. She knew that she was not in a position to risk another heartbreak at this stage. If she allowed greater proximity with Rishaan, she knew she'd find it difficult to keep herself emotionally detached.

But, was she still unaffected? She didn't quite have an answer except that, at times, she really missed Rishaan in office and wanted to chat with him more often than they usually did. In fact, she found it strange that he didn't feel the same way.

Rishaan, on the other hand, felt quite the same way. He not just wanted to chat with her more often, but also wanted to spend more time with her. He found her sudden detachment very strange.

Therefore, instead of accelerating the romance, Kiara and Rishaan held themselves back a bit, consciously so, and without verbalizing the reverse move. They needed some time off to settle into their new professional roles as well. So, for the next two weeks they met outside over dinners every second night. This was the only time they could manage, given that Kiara was often held up in the office till late evenings.

Two weeks later, one night after they had dinner, Kiara asked Rishaan if she could spend the night at his place since Rimi's parents had come to Mumbai for a day and there was a lot of disturbance at her house.

Fact was that Kiara wasn't best friends with her roommate, Rimi; they stayed together only to reduce their individual share of rent. Therefore, Kiara did not feel comfortable asking Rishaan to come to her place late in the night.

Rishaan, for his part, had asked her twice to come home with him after dinner, but she had avoided on the pretext of being tired.

Nonetheless, Rishaan gladly relented to her request this time round.

That night, as Rishaan and Kiara lay on bed holding each

other, Rishaan played out the collection of his favourite Hindi movie songs. Kiara liked old Hindi songs just as much, except those by the legendary singer Mukesh. In fact, she mentioned this in passing and rather matter-of-factly. Rishaan absorbed the information as casually as he could, and made no effort to find out the reason for the specific avoidance.

They lay, still and calm, clasped gently on to each other, soaking in the ethereal joy of R.D. Burman's timeless masterpieces. As a 1978 song 'Phir Wahi Raat Hai' from the Rekha–Vinod Mehra starrer, *Ghar,* played out, it produced a rare and magical mutual sensation of physical oneness.

Rishaan and Kiara played the song over and over again. They floated in its mystical lyrics, letting their natural instincts and urges take over. They made love, the experience as passionate and out-of-the-world as it could ever be.

The two week 'physical' ceasefire between them now stood broken.

Soon after, Rishaan dozed off while Kiara was left alone negotiating her conundrums. She hated herself for not being able to control her feelings. But why did she want to control something that seemed so natural? Was she being too hard on herself? Was she being unfair to Rishaan just because of her obnoxious experience with someone else?

Kiara finally dozed off two hours later and got up when the first ray of light sneaked into their room around 6 a.m. Rishaan was still fast asleep. She got up and looked around the house. The place was untidy; the utensils and food were scattered all around in the kitchen. She came back to his room and opened his cupboard. Things weren't any better there as well. Everything was crammed into it in the most haphazard way.

Rishaan surely seemed a disorganized guy on the home front. She took a deep breath and started arranging his cupboard. The cupboard done, she shifted stuff around in the kitchen to give it a tidier look. After this tedious exercise, she prepared herself a black coffee and came back to the bedroom. Kiara slowly sipped her coffee sitting by Rishaan's side, looking at him and thinking about their strange relationship. While Rishaan was still asleep, she gently kissed him on the forehead and left for home, realizing that she would need an hour to reach, get ready and leave for office.

When Rishaan woke up an hour later, he was pleasantly surprised to see his abode look so neat and tidy. The first thought to cross his mind was that Kiara would perhaps make a great homemaker as well, a side of her he had not seen yet. But why did she have to go off so abruptly without telling him? Was she still unaffected by what had happened the previous night?

That evening Rishaan picked her up from office.

'Why did you have to come all the way?' she asked him surprised.

In her heart of hearts though, she wanted to hear him profess his love to her.

'Why did you have to clean up my house?' he asked instead.

'My wish,' she answered.

'It's my wish then that we spend another night together.'

Kiara wanted to avoid going back to his place so soon. But since, she was chumming, she knew it would be a safe night. Much to her surprise, even Rishaan preferred to chat, prepare dinner together, watch some TV and doze off.

For the next three weeks or so, Rishaan and Kiara behaved very much like a couple without formalizing their 'relationship status'.

As rational thinkers, they were not sure about the longevity of their relationship and whether at all it would reach the stage of marriage. But for now, this did not bother them. What made them feel good and positive about the future was that their feelings were genuine and mutual. Guarded optimism seemed to be propelling them ahead.

As Rishaan and Kiara started spending more nights and weekends together, apart from their intense chemistry, they also became privy to those traits that they didn't like in each other.

For instance, Rishaan found her too 'career-obsessed' at times. As a 'creative' freelancer, there were times when he'd feel low and would want to talk about his anxieties or simply discuss a new idea he had cracked. Due to Kiara's hectic work schedule, he invariably wouldn't find her by his side when he needed her the most. When he thought about it logically, he knew that Kiara couldn't be blamed for it, but again at the given moment, it left him lonely and depressed.

The other thing that irked him was her obsession with the BBM. He discovered that one of her best buddies, Mohit, was in fact her ex-boyfriend.

'We were seeing each other for a year when I was in my first year of college. He was in the third year then. We had some very peculiar idiosyncrasies and soon realized that we'd be better off as best buddies instead,' Kiara had once told Rishaan with her usual candour.

'What does he do now?'

'He works with an advertising firm in Delhi. You know,

whenever he faces a relationship crisis, he knows that the best counsel will come from me,' she boasted. 'I have never seen a more finicky guy than him. We now laugh at the thought that we were seeing each other at one point of time,' she chucked.

Rishaan wasn't sure how to react to this.

'Can an ex-boyfriend be a good friend and confidant?' he asked diffidently.

'Why not? Don't they know you better than most other people? Besides, in life some people are destined to be around in your life, in one form or another,' she replied with her usual aplomb.

To add to the list, Rishaan didn't quite like Kiara's smoking habit: six to ten cigarettes a day depending upon mood and company. And that he often found himself allergic to the exhaled smoke worsened the situation. Kiara was aware about it. She had indeed reduced smoking in front of him but otherwise was unapologetic about the habit. Was he being too demanding in expecting her to change for him? And more so, at this stage when their relationship was undefined?

Rishaan decided to cast his doubts away. Yes, Kiara seemed more rebellious and fiercely independent than any other girl he had met. But she also seemed nakedly honest. Why would she otherwise tell him that the guy she was chatting with late-night on the BBM helping him sort out some issues was her ex-boyfriend?

Rishaan concluded that Kiara was probably more sorted than he was, and that for best results he would have to give her adequate space to be the way she was.

As for Kiara, she too had her set of problems. She did not like that Rishaan lived in his own idealistic, dreamy world that was often at loggerheads with the world outside. He was spontaneous, talented and great fun to be with, but could also be extremely disorganized both at home and on the professional front. Kiara thought herself to be more money-wise than him. She felt his decision to foray as an independent scriptwriter wasn't backed by a solid business plan. This was a concept Rishaan did not relate with at all.

'Money flows naturally when you do what you are most happy doing,' Rishaan would say, in defence of his decision to quit his job and pursue an uncertain future.

'On the contrary, you're most happy when there is a good flow of money,' she'd say, articulating her viewpoint.

'Which means you'll be in a job-like situation all your life?'

'I don't know, but I live for the present. And right now, I am enjoying it.'

'Oh...and I live aspiring for the future!'

Hence, while Kiara was sceptical of Rishaan's nomadic streak, Rishaan had his doubts about her materialistic propensities. Of course, every time they met, the intense natural chemistry they felt for each other decimated these vague doubts until a certain incident made them resurface. By and large, though, they seemed happy being in each other's company. A guarded, unspoken, mutual optimism kept making the partnership stronger, even though both of them consciously employed some self-regulations to prevent themselves from going public or overboard.

And then, one day, circumstances conspired to end the status quo!

When Kiara met Rishaan on a Saturday evening, she looked hassled and tensed. The previous night, her roommate was arrested in a police raid from a rave party which was taking place in a Juhu hotel. Post that, the landlord had served her an ultimatum: Vacate the house in the next three days.

'Gosh! What did I do? I barely knew that girl for the last six months. This is such ridiculous luck!' she rued.

'Hmm... So what are you going to do now?'

'No idea,' she shook her head.

'Move in with me.'

Rishaan made the offer, fairly confident that Kiara would have no reason to reject it.

'Nah! Bad idea.' She shook her head.

'Why?' Rishaan asked, taken aback by the unexpected answer.

'You must be kidding. I can be with you for a few days until I find a new accommodation. But living in... No.'

Kiara prevented herself from explaining further. After some thought, she had changed her mind.

'No, just chuck it. Tomorrow is Sunday and I will utilize the full day to find myself a new accommodation.'

Rishaan was visibly hurt by her unreasonable distancing.

'Waiter. Get me the check please,' said he abruptly.

An uneasy silence dotted their journey when Rishaan dropped her back home.

That night, both Rishaan and Kiara were inundated with doubts that refused to leave them alone.

'Why did Kiara have a problem shifting in with me? Is this really a transitory, stop-gap relationship for her?' Rishaan wondered hurtfully.

'Is Rishaan like most other men who just want to rush into a live-in arrangement or does he intend to go beyond? If he does, then why hasn't he hinted yet for a commitment?' she wondered confused.

It was a restless and lonely Saturday night for both.

Early Sunday morning, Rishaan was woken up by the jarring noise of the doorbell. He dragged himself out of bed and hardly had he opened the door than he found Kiara standing at the doorstep.

'Rishaan, I need to talk to you about something,' said she.

Rishaan looked at her in anticipation...

'Would you care to define our relationship?' she asked directly. Her words had an uncanny resemblance to those of his. 'Hadn't he asked her the same question a few weeks ago,' he thought.

'Come inside.'

Rishaan took a moment to think and then went inside to his room. He returned carrying a beautifully wrapped box.

'Would you mind changing into this?' he asked her with a poker face.

'What's this?' Kiara asked, confused.

'It's your birthday gift. I wanted to gift you this dress three weeks later on your birthday. But now I want you to wear this.'

'But Rishaan, I have asked you an important question. Don't trivialize it.'

'Just do as I say. You will get all your answers today.' He remained firm.

Kiara relented reluctantly and went inside to change. When she opened the gift wrap and saw the gift, she had no idea how she should react. Five minutes later, Kiara walked out in a trendy, black lingerie. She was visibly annoyed but still brazen. Rishaan was surprised to see her actually don it.

'So aren't you ready to click me?' she asked tauntingly.

'Wow. You wore it? You look gorgeous,' he gushed.

'Yeah I did because I need to understand your psyche today. Is sex the only thing that's for real between us? I need to know,' she asked him rather pointedly.

Rishaan shook his head, remaining cool and casual.

'Define our relationship, Rishaan,' she demanded.

All of a sudden, Rishaan bent down on his knees, held her hands and took her by surprise.

'I love you. I love you, Kiara,' he proposed looking straight into her eyes. 'And I want to love you all my life.'

These magical words left Kiara overwhelmed. And yet she had no clue why she had to be proposed in the awkwardness of being draped with just these three tiny triangles. 'Does that define our relationship?' he asked her. She bent down and kissed him passionately. After a wet lip-lock, her first query was: 'But why on earth did I have to be proposed like this?' Rishaan explained that he always had this fantasy to propose to his girlfriend after getting her to wear the world's sexiest lingerie.

Kiara loved Rishaan for these crazy surprises. In as much as she was conscious of their temperamental differences, she was also aware that it were these differences that actually kept pushing them closer.

That evening Kiara shifted in with Rishaan. With this live-in arrangement, their relationship status had changed overnight. The next morning, their friends on Facebook were the first to notice the change. Rishaan and Kiara were now 'In a relationship'.

Seven

> *Find what you love and let it kill you.*
> —CHARLES BUKOWSKI

At every stage of a romantic relationship the equation between a man and a woman changes. In the early days of getting to know each other, everything that's aberrant or unusual in your partner, seems fascinating. As the couple gets closer, often those very things which they loved in their partner, begins to turn them off. There are usually two reasons for this: one, with greater proximity, there is a greater sense of belongingness towards the partner, as also a formal ownership which is recognized by the society. Hence, the aberrant/rebellious/bohemian ways of your partner, which seemed so tantalizing until sometime ago, suddenly carries the risk of causing embarrassment. Two, most individuals want their partner to form some sort of a cohesive arrangement that ensures peaceful coexistence between them. A hint of disapproval towards specific traits of each other, coupled with dearth of mutual respect, often leads to a dicey situation in which the partner finds it difficult to remain unaffected.

Kiara woke up to her first morning as Rishaan's flatmate and living-in partner, brimming with a rare feeling of positivity.

Stretching herself, she got out of bed and looked outside their seventh-floor window. Had it been a floor higher, one could get a direct view of the sea. Nonetheless, she soaked in the lovely sea breeze before getting ready for office. Rishaan remained asleep until the maid, Laxmi bai, rang the bell.

As they chatted over a quick breakfast, Kiara acquainted Rishaan with her ideas for the house.

'You know what, Rishaan, the house needs painting. This common beige colour across all rooms looks too plain and monotonous. Let's plan this. We can paint the living room in grey and white with a few patches of orange here and there. The inside room could be of a more sober colour like azure blue with a white roof.' Rishaan, who was still groggy, heard her out somewhat disinterestedly, even as Kiara went on, 'I think the curtains need to be changed. They seem too old. In fact, why do you need curtains at all in your living room? Since this doubles up as your office, I think you should go for the venetian blinds. They give such an elegant office look.'

'No...no... I like it this way. The windows open, the breeze blowing in,' a resistant Rishaan exclaimed.

'Oh come on, Rishaan. Just visualize it. I will change the lighting as well. Instead of this regular tubelight, I'll get you a well-designed spotlight which will be positioned right above your work station and a lamp for that corner. In fact, get rid of this old-sarkari-office-type computer table also. Let's get something sleeker for you to work on.'

Kiara was very excited about her idea and instantly checked out for venetian blinds shops on her mobile internet. She located one in Lokhandwala and suggested they check out the shop in the evening itself. By now, Rishaan was feeling a bit irritated by her persuasive behaviour. He tried changing the topic but when that did not happen, he decided that he had to be more blunt.

'Listen, Kiara, I like the natural light of this room and prefer to keep the windows open at all times. Can I please retain it this way? After all, I'm the one who will be spending most of the time here.'

Kiara was a bit taken aback by the firmness in Rishaan's tenor. She looked at her watch and took his leave.

'Listen Kiara, I am sorry. You know that I appreciate your inputs but at times, I like to have it my way,' Rishaan tried reasoning out with her.

'It's fine, Rishaan. We have a long way to go and it makes sense for both of us to understand and respect each other's preferences,' she smiled.

Kiara gave him a peck on his cheeks, hugged him and left for work. She was definitely a bit hurt. Later, Rishaan thought about their conversation. He was glad that she wanted to be 'involved' in his life and his choices. Didn't this augur well for their future? Shouldn't he have actually allowed her to have her way? He wasn't sure.

With a new occupant in the house, the existing system underwent some changes. The expenses were to be shared and responsibilities divided. Having grown up in laidback Lucknow, Rishaan was accustomed to living in more spacious houses than most people in Mumbai lived in. Hence, two years ago, despite some financial constraints, he, along with a flatmate had opted for a two bedroom house instead of one. Six months ago, his flatmate had got married and since then Rishaan was bearing a humongous rent of ₹32,000 all alone. Hence, even though he never showed this in front of Kiara, her shifting in with him was a huge financial relief for him. He had anyways been looking for a partner. He wasn't expecting himself to be so lucky as to find one, who apart from sharing the rent, would share his bed.

Life seemed exciting. He wasn't complaining any more.

As a basic plan, it was decided that apart from sharing rent, Rishaan would take care of the grocery expenses while Kiara would pay the maid and electricity bills. On weekdays, Rishaan would decide the food menu, while on weekends, Kiara would have her way. Kiara preferred a more English breakfast—stuff like muesli, porridge and other health food. Rishaan was more desi in his preferences. Rishaan sometimes playfully taunted her that the effects of her 'healthy breakfast' were getting blown away with every puff of cigarette she exhaled. Until one day she gifted him an imported deodorant and reminded him that since she didn't comment upon his choice of cheap-priced toiletries and deodorants, she didn't appreciate him commenting on her personal choices either. Rishaan wasn't sure if the two things could really be equated. One indeed involved personal choice; the other involved her health. But he knew that arguing with a free-spirited woman was often not a great thing to do. As for Kiara, she had got the cue and would mostly go to the other room to smoke.

For the next few weeks, both Rishaan and Kiara had very demanding work schedules. Rishaan had narrated his script to the renowned Bollywood director, Aakash Jha, who had carved a niche for himself as the director of some of Bollywood's best political thrillers. Jha quite liked the script, but, like all top directors, he had a slightly different vision. Hence, Jha suggested that the story be tweaked in a certain way before it could be narrated to his favourite star, Ravi Dewan. Given the time constraints, and that Jha's suggestions involved additional research and a good amount of reworking of the script, Rishaan was extremely busy for the next three weeks. Kiara, on the other hand, got busy with her own project that required market research for the new channel. As part of field research to ascertain viewer preferences, she even had to travel to three SEC-B cities—Nagpur, Baroda and Indore. And once she was back, her detailed research report had to be shared and discussed with the programming team.

Hence, due to their hectic schedules for almost a month, Kiara and Rishaan hardly spent any quality time together. There were days when Kiara would come back home only around midnight, they'd chat for some time and then while Kiara, tired and worn out, would doze off, Rishaan would work till 4 in the morning. Sex, which had been the most uplifting part of their relationship, had taken a back seat. One night when they managed some time out and had just gotten into the act, they faced the most unexpected deterrent. There was a loud quarrel between the two neighbouring families. The fight, which started over one of the neighbour's pet dog defecating in front of other neighbour's door, eventually escalated to a point where the police was called in and as witness, Rishaan too was questioned. By the time Rishaan freed himself, Kiara was already fast asleep. Hard luck it was!

Despite their super busy schedule, Kiara and Rishaan felt good about this whole feeling of coming back to somebody. They were getting a bit restless, though, waiting for that elusive weekend when they would not be burdened by work and would have more time for each other.

The wait ended soon. Rishaan was done with the reworking of his script, and was waiting for an appointment with the director. Kiara too was on the verge of finalizing the marketing strategy for two of the most crucial prime-time shows of the new channel. They finally had at their disposal a weekend, where work wouldn't be the spoilsport between them.

It was the third Saturday of April and last few days had been unusually tepid. Rishaan and Kiara had had a heavy brunch and were lazing around in the living room, drinking chilled beer and watching a movie.

All of a sudden, Kiara turned to Rishaan and said, 'Rishaan, the last few weeks have bored me to death. Let's do something exciting, na.'

'Any suggestions?'

'Ah...well...something we haven't done yet.'

Rishaan weighed the options and a naughty smile brightened his face.

'Hey, listen, I have a fantastic idea. We'll go out of the city. Just pack your bag. I'll give you my stuff as well.'

'But where are we going?'

'That will be a surprise.'

As they packed their stuff, Rishaan and Kiara felt a peculiar sense of excitement, one that precedes an escapade. To make this one live up to the other truly magical experiences they'd had, Rishaan suggested that both Kiara and he must come up with a super crazy surprise only to be disclosed at night.

Three hours later, just before sunset, Rishaan drove Kiara into a resort which was built at the highest point of Lonavala, a hill station almost equidistant from Mumbai and Pune. It seemed like Paradise on earth, with clouds surrounding it from all sides. This was the most beautiful place that Kiara had ever seen in her life. After checking in, they quickly rushed to the fenced edge of the resort to get the best view of the setting sun.

'Gosh! This is so beautiful. I can't imagine something as gorgeous as this exists so close to Mumbai,' she gushed in joy.

'It's indeed awesome. I didn't know it will actually be this good.'

'Oh, you haven't been here before?' she asked him, surprised. 'Then how did you know about this place?'

'Well, from the internet. You know that I'm dreamy. I had been searching for places I'd go to with my girlfriend. Now that I have one, I thought I might as well begin the journey.'

Kiara was deeply touched by these words. She held his hand gently as both turned towards the setting sun to savour the last few moments of dusk. Soon, it was dark and the temperature began to dip. Rishaan and Kiara chatted by the poolside, sipping wine and followed it with an early dinner.

'Oh, I forgot it's gonna be a long night, right?' Kiara said, remembering they had a 'surprise-throwing' thing later at night.

An hour later, Kiara and Rishaan were in their room kissing and feeling each other, until Rishaan pulled himself away.

'So what's your surprise?' Rishaan asked her.

'What's yours?'

'You reveal yours first because mine will take up a lot of time.'

Kiara made Rishaan learn a skill he had never hoped he would. She made him wax her legs. She spelt out the instructions at once and then lied down, leaving her lower body entirely to Rishaan's discretion. To her surprise, Rishaan was rather skilled at the job, at times giving the impression that he wouldn't mind pursuing the task professionally.

The act bred a sense of intimacy that was irresistibly seductive and plain erotic. No wonder that by the time he was done, he found it difficult to control his testosterone. They made love, rather impulsively and then lay on the bed for a long time, holding each other.

'So, are you ready with your surprise?' Kiara asked him.

Rishaan's impish smile gave Kiara the ample hint that he had planned something unimaginably crazy.

Fifteen minutes later, Rishaan and Kiara were in the swimming pool, the only two people to be there at midnight. The water was cold, making Kiara shiver. But Rishaan looked determined to brave the adversity.

'Rishaan, are you crazy? What are we doing here? Come, let's go back,' said Kiara, battling the discomfort.

'Wasn't I supposed to do something really crazy?' he reiterated, with an unaffected naughy smile.

'I want us to make love in the swimming pool. This is one of my biggest fantasies,' he finally divulged his plan.

'Whattt?'

Fifteen minutes later, when they had almost done it, a better sense of civic responsibility intervened the act and prevented them from going all out. 'Let's continue inside. It won't be fair for the other guests who use the pool tomorrow morning,' reasoned Kiara. They completed the act in the bathtub of their room, with silken-white foam-filled water adjusted to the right degree of warm and the sweet smell of lavender-dipped-candles enveloping the air.

The hangover of the crazy Saturday night kept them lost in thought throughout their journey back home.

♦

On Monday morning when Kiara and Rishaan were back to work, they couldn't concentrate on work all day. The one hell of an experience they had over the weekend had left a hangover that was very powerful. Kiara seemed more affected. She was suddenly missing Rishaan like never before. She messaged him at least a dozen times from office, at times talking about the weekend's experience and other times simply enquiring about his writing or if he had had his meal. The answers were mostly cryptic, which she found a bit surprising.

Rishaan, for his part, was surely distracted by the weekend's hangover. But he also wanted to quickly get over it and get his concentration back on work. On Friday, he was supposed to narrate his script to Aakash Jha. This would be a make-or-break opportunity of sorts for him, considering the amount of effort and time he had invested in the script. If the film happened, it would kick-start his career as scriptwriter of movies. If not, he might have to explore stuff that weren't his first preference.

Rishaan's distraction had him probe himself deep. He wondered if work was the only reason why he wanted to play down the weekend's experience. Or if it was something about Kiara that wasn't yet giving him the confidence that their relationship was for a lifetime?

Rishaan found his thoughts vague. They could simply be the creation of a lonely mind. But he knew that he wasn't yet feeling the same natural propensities that he felt a couple of month ago, to now take his relationship with Kiara to the next level.

Was it the uncertainty of his professional career that was making him go slow? Did it have something to do with Kiara? Or was he just enjoying the comfort zone that Kiara and he were in right now?

He deduced that it could possibly be a little bit of all three.

Eight

> *A kiss is a lovely trick designed by nature to stop speech when words become superfluous.*
> —INGRID BERGMAN

When things are good, they're great. When they are bad, they can turn into a disaster.

It is strange that at one stage one craves for proximity and at the very next one wants space. Rishaan had begun to realize that there were certain things about Kiara that he just could not bear. For instance, when the teenaged delivery boy from the local grocery shop rang the doorbell early in the morning, Kiara would open the door wearing her micro-sized shorts. And the moment she turned around to get the money, the boy would ogle at her legs in a rather starving way.

'Kiara, would you mind putting on your pyjama when you open the door early mornings?' Rishaan advised her, rather curtly one morning. 'I don't like the way the guy stares at your legs.'

Kiara who was preoccupied typing a message on her cell, nodded casually. However, the inherent rebel in her continued doing what she wanted. A week later, when Rishaan stepped out for a meeting around noon, one of the building lifts had been shut down for repairs while the other remained occupied for the next few minutes. He therefore had to walk down the seven floors. Halfway through, he heard two male-voices murmuring in the staircase. He grew suspicious and started walking more stealthily to find out who they were. He saw the grocery shop delivery-boy and the building watchman sitting on the stairs. Since Rishaan was behind them, they had not seen him yet. The teenaged delivery-boy was busy showing the middle-aged watchman a couple of pictures he had clicked on his low-end cellphone camera. The pictures, apparently, were of a woman occupying one of the flats. As the delivery boy raved about the *'mast maal* on the 7th floor' and claimed that *'main to uspe poori tarah fida hoon!'*, Rishaan instantly knew who she was. He descended on the men with a loud thud and swiftly snatched the cellphone. He was stunned to see pictures of Kiara's legs exposed. A livid Rishaan trashed the delivery boy's phone on the floor and slapped him non-stop about a dozen times, employing invectives, which he had not used in a very long time. The delivery boy barely managed to flee. Before Rishaan could vent his ire on the watchman, an uncle staying in the building joined the scene. Upon knowing about what had happened, a septuagenarian uncle who had a knack for rubbing people the wrong way with his acerbic comments, had a piece of advice for Rishaan: 'If you leave your jewellery exposed to thieves, they will attempt to steal it.' That evening, Kiara and Rishaan had a major skirmish.

'Listen Kiara, you got to be careful with what you wear when you open the door or go for your jogs,' Rishaan ordered her.

'Oh come on, Rishaan. These people are uneducated and have no outlook. But why are you talking like them?'

'Kiara, try and understand what I am saying. We live with these perverts all around us. I don't want someone to grope you and then...'

'Rape me?'

'I'm glad you understand. Just look at what's happening all around. We can't change the world, but women can be a bit careful. And that's not in the least to say that I am dictating what you should be wearing. You're free to wear whatever you want to, but in a place that is conducive to wear them. I hope I make sense.'

Kiara agreed to be more careful. It was not that Rishaan wasn't making any sense to her. 'But, why did he have to bother about things that didn't really concern him?' she thought. Rishaan, on the other hand, was left wondering why even the simplest of things had to be debated and argued with Kiara.

Kiara had no interest in cooking. Having stayed in a boarding school and then in college hostels, she was used to her meals being prepared by others. She somehow didn't feel the need to turn things around even now. As such, she seldom managed to get the right mix of sugar, tea leaves and milk in the tea she prepared. The only thing she could cook well was Maggi noodles, which she was quite proud of. Kiara's disinterest in the kitchen, would at times bug Rishaan. Was he not within his rights to expect that she prepare a cup of tea for him, at least on a weekend? Rishaan was gracious not to talk to her about this, but he wished Kiara would show a greater sense of belongingness in shouldering responsibilities. Kiara, for her part, was deliberately a bit complacent in contributing to household chores after being snubbed for her suggestions to change the look of the living room.

Fortunately, for a couple of weeks, the two were a bit relaxed on the work front. Rishaan's narration to the director had gotten postponed as the director was unwell; on the other hand, the launch of Kiara's channel had been delayed for some time to make space for some distribution deals. The relaxation on the professional front allowed them to get back to what was undoubtedly the highpoint of their relationship: frequent, passionate sex. They would engage in it almost every night!

Gymming together also helped them break out of that wee bit of monotony that was beginning to creep into their lives. Every morning at 6, they worked out together for an hour before proceeding with their professional engagements. While Rishaan would focus on weight training, Kiara was more into spinning and group exercises. Rishaan would approach his session at the gym with the same single-minded focus with which he did other things; Kiara on the other hand, would utilize opportunities of networking as well. 'For a marketing person, there's no limit to networking. You never know who is going to get you the next big deal,' she'd say rather upfront, a concept Rishaan could never relate with.

One day after Rishaan was done with his session, he went out looking for Kiara. She was seated at the café, with a good-looking hunk. They seemed to have known each other.

'Hey Rishaan, meet Piyush. I just met him at our spinning session. He owns a recruitment agency that specializes in media jobs.'

Rishaan and Piyush exchanged formal pleasantries. Soon after, Piyush surprised Rishaan by inviting him home.

'So do we catch up this Saturday? Actually, I'm throwing a small house-party for my close friends. Why don't you guys join me?' said Piyush.

Confused, Rishaan looked at Kiara for a cue.

'Well, this weekend we will be in Delhi,' replied Rishaan, making his disapproval to this 'fast-track' friendship pretty obvious.

On their way back home, Kiara raved about her new contact.

'You know what, Piyush was telling me that he can get me a job in one of the competing channels for almost 1.5 times of what I am getting here.'

Rishaan did not encourage the conversation further.

'I think you should first settle in this job and do your bit which can make you feel proud of your contribution. At this moment, I don't see a point in hopping jobs like a vagabond.'

Kiara did not see a point in debating on this any further. By now, both she and Rishaan had a sense of what topics they should not argue on. Their temperamental differences notwithstanding, they continued to have a terrific physical chemistry.

The first major crack in their relationship surfaced two weeks later and unfortunately coincided with Kiara's birthday.

Rishaan obviously wanted to make the day super special. On the evening preceding her birthday, he decorated the house all by himself, getting twenty-four large-sized bouquets of red roses, each dedicated to the year of her life gone by. He had even baked a chocolate rum–cake by downloading the recipe from the internet. Post the mini-celebration at home, he had planned to drive her to somewhere beautiful.

At 8 in the evening, the time Kiara was usually back home from office, he got a call from her.

'Rishaan, listen I am stuck. The CEO has called us for a meeting to Lower Parel and I don't think I can be back until 11 or so.'

Rishaan was quite upset. He wasn't sure whether he had the right to be so, considering he hadn't mentioned the plan to Kiara. Perhaps he had expected her to sound a bit apologetic, which she clearly didn't.

That evening after CEO reprimanded the marketing team on a couple of issues, the Marketing head held a separate meeting with his team which went on well past midnight. And by the time, Kiara returned home, Rishaan had dozed off. Without switching on the lights of the living room, an exhausted Kiara went to bed.

It was only next morning when Kiara stepped into the living room that she realized the efforts Rishaan had invested in making her birthday special. Rishaan sat there reading the newspaper and wished her rather formally. He couldn't hide his disappointment.

Kiara was simply floored to look at the rose bouquets. She hugged Rishaan spontaneously and the two were engaged in a passionate embrace for some time. Rishaan surprised Kiara with her birthday gift: a sparkling, black, uber-hot party-gown. Kiara simply loved it and grabbed Rishaan for a passionate kiss. They'd have gone further had it not been for the maid's inopportune doorbell.

In as much as Kiara wanted to spend the day with Rishaan, she had to leave for work. She promised to take him out for dinner that evening.

The whole day Kiara kept receiving birthday messages and calls from her friends and colleagues. She was conscious though of not having been wished by that one person who, for the past five years, had always been the first to wish her: her best buddy, Ajit.

Ajit finally called her at 6, only to give her a surprise.

'Hey Kiara, listen I've just landed in Mumbai to celebrate your birthday. Where are you?'

Ajit was supposed to take a flight to London from Mumbai at 1:30 in the morning. Since the day coincided with Kiara's birthday, whom he had not met since college, he planned to meet her in person. Ajit's call to Kiara put her in an unnecessary quandary. She knew Rishaan wasn't the sort of boyfriend who would like meeting her ex. But then, should she be rude to her best buddy, who had stood by her through thick and thin?

Two hours later, Rishaan, Kiara and Ajit sat over dinner at a suburban Chinese restaurant. Rishaan was visibly awkward, and even though Ajit made an extra effort to humour him, it made very little difference. After the spoilt last evening, the last thing Rishaan wanted was to meet Kiara's ex on her birthday. But courtesy to some peculiar situations that demand a basic formality, Rishaan acceded to the idea of a threesome dinner.

Notwithstanding his personal displeasure, Rishaan was beginning to feel that Ajit was perhaps a good, jovial bloke.

'So what's taking you to London?' Rishaan asked Ajit.

'My girlfriend.'

Ajit unabashedly confessed that since he had recently broken up for the fourth time, within a span of two years, instead of brooding he had decided to celebrate the break-up.

He added that two of his other friends were to join him in London, and all of them together would spend a fortnight having 'fun'.

Rishaan wondered what the emphasis on 'fun' really meant. Four break-ups in two years anyway meant he was perhaps just having fun.

Ajit, like Kiara, had a big appetite for alcohol, way bigger than Rishaan. And once he got a bit high, he eased up with Rishaan. Rishaan did not appreciate his blabbering anymore. But Ajit was so drunk by then that he was barely conscious of himself. There was a point when Kiara stepped out for a bit to go to the washroom, leaving the two men alone. For a minute or two, Ajit and Rishaan struggled to make conversation, until Ajit broke the ice.

'Rishaan, dude, you are lucky to have a partner like Kiara. I've been with many women but if there is someone I regret losing, it's Kiara,' he blabbered, intoxication slurring his words.

'Yeah, I know you've experienced her enough,' Rishaan said, rather sarcastically. 'So you want to get her back, is it?'

A sheepish, awkward smile was all that he could offer for an answer. 'Well, I'm sure you would have realized by now that with Kiara, its only and only about her. The partner has very little say in the relationship. She chose to move on, not me. I wish she was less transient.'

The word 'transient' felt like a low-blow to Rishaan. And before he could react, Kiara came back. The evening ended soon after as Ajit had to rush to the international airport. Kiara offered Ajit a drop off, but sensing that Rishaan wasn't in the best of moods, Ajit insisted to go on his own.

That night, when Rishaan and Kiara were driving back home, for the first time they seemed to have nothing to talk about. An unexpected, pre-monsoon shower had made the weather very pleasant but it had no effect on Rishaan's temper. The last conversation with Ajit kept playing in his mind. Kiara, for her part, was just too tired, to realize that something was bothering Rishaan.

To distract himself, Rishaan turned on the radio. A beautiful song of the legendary singer, Mukesh, was playing on one of the channels, which made him feel slightly better. Hardly had he started to enjoy the song when Kiara changed the channel to an English song she wanted to hear. Peeved, Rishaan immediately switched the radio back to his channel. And when Kiara changed it again to her's, Rishaan burst out.

'What the f***ing hell is this, Kiara? Why is that that everything between us has to be about you? Do my preferences matter to you at all?' he yelled.

For a moment, Kiara was shocked. But she instantly gathered herself.

'Why have you started talking like Ajit? These are precisely his words and he'd use them so often that I couldn't take them anymore.'

'And you moved on?'

Kiara wondered what had suddenly gone wrong between them. Wasn't it eerie that out of nowhere an unsuspecting conversation between her and Rishaan had replicated an unfortunate situation she had once experienced with Ajit?

As they struggled to make conversation, Kiara told him rather irritatedly, 'Listen Rishaan, will you just stop this Mukesh song for now? I cannot understand how you and

Ajit have similar choices. We've had many fights over these melancholic songs. The memory just disturbs me.'

'If it still disturbs you so much, it means you're not over the person completely. Then, why the hell did you to meet him?'

At that point Rishaan almost banged his car into a lorry passing by. They managed a lucky, close-shave.

'Can you stop the car and then fight, if you have to?'

Rishaan brought the car to a rough halt.

'Why did you have to meet Ajit, if his thoughts still bother you?' he asked her in a more punctuated, pointed tone.

'I didn't, damn it. He called me out of the blue and it would have been discourteous if I refused to meet him on my birthday. And I moved on from him long, long ago'

'Why? Are there some special memories of the way you celebrated it with him?'

'You sound sick.'

'Oh! Really? I sound sick? By the way, your ex-boyfriend still regrets breaking up with you.'

'I don't.'

'Maybe, yes. Because your choices are generally transient.'

When Kiara head the word 'transient', she was convinced that a conversation with Ajit in her absence was making Rishaan behave in this rather strange manner. She remembered it quite well that in all their skirmishes, Ajit would repeat certain words, and it was nothing short of weird that Rishaan had unknowingly used pretty much the same words. She decided not to prolong the argument and took it upon herself to reassure Rishaan.

'Listen, Rishaan, I am not transient. I know my mind

better than most other people.'

'Oh, really? What do you know about yourself?'

A tense pause preceded Kiara's answer.

'At least...that I love you and I want to be with you all my life.'

Kiara's last words shook Rishaan. It gave him an idea of how many different layers a contemporary woman could carry compatibly enough and simultaneously so, in her personality. He was overwhelmed. In a voice flooded with emotions, but one which somehow lacked the same conviction as Kiara's, Rishaan reciprocated mellow, 'I love you too.'

A sudden burst of shower, timed to perfection, created just the right ambience for Rishaan and Kiara to do what came most naturally to them—a lip-lock. Kiara slid her hand past his arms and switched to the channel playing Mukesh's songs.

Nine

Love is an untamed force. When we try to control it, it destroys us. When we try to imprison it, it enslaves us. When we try to understand it, it leaves us feeling lost and confused.
—PAULO COELHO

Rishaan tried hard to put all the thoughts and notions about Kiara into perspective. He was fairly reassured that she loved him and genuinely so. At least that's what her assertion—*I love you and I want to be with you all my life*—had him think. Kiara, however, was a habitual rebel and also partially selfish. But so what? Was he sure that he never came across as being selfish?

In fact, as Rishaan mulled over his relationship with Kiara, he realized that there were two specific factors that had made modern relationships more testing than ever before. The first revolved around a largely consumerist mindset which almost everybody around seemed to be affected with. For instance, why did this generation have to compulsively remain 'connected' 24x7 either via Facebook, Twitter, WhatsApp, BBM or in most cases all of the four? Would this humongous volume of social connectivity leave you with any time, interest or motivation to nurture personal bonds?

Secondly, the modern woman is a huge challenge. She hates the chauvinistic attitudes that most men still carry because she knows she is capable of all that a man is capable of. She is possessive about her independence. She has a fair sense of discerning the right from the wrong. She absolutely abhors it when her 'liberated' self is subjected to moral scrutiny. And when she falls in love, she gives it her all, but on her terms, which often makes the man perceive her as selfish. Well, wasn't this complicated? For Rishaan, it was!

Rishaan realized that the challenge for him was to come to terms with Kiara's dichotomous self. For this, he would have to let go of his own rigidness. He perhaps needed to stop thinking about their relationship and simply enjoy the moment. In other words, he must chill and relax a bit.

Since Kiara had come out of a traumatic relationship, she had consciously kept her expectations low. She hoped for the best while keeping herself prepared for anything.

With some sort of clarity in his thoughts, Rishaan got down to finalizing his reworked script. The director, Aakash Jha, had recovered from his illness and could call him for a narration anytime. And so it was, that Thursday night Jha called Rishaan and asked if he could give a narration on the coming Saturday morning. Rishaan grabbed the opportunity!

The whole of Friday was spent making some last minute changes to the script. By the evening, he was feeling damn nervous and wished if only he could narrate it to someone. He wasn't sure if Kiara would be the right person to whom he should narrate the script, for she had never shown the kind of interest in his scripts that would make him feel confident of seeking her feedback. But for want of option, he ended up calling Kiara, then in office. Kiara instantly agreed for the narration, her excitement pleasantly surprising Rishaan.

Over midnight coffee Rishaan narrated his script to Kiara, in the very same Novotel Hotel sofa which they had occupied on the fateful night that changed the course of their lives. Kiara tried being as attentive as she could be, but given that it had been a long, tedious week for her, she really struggled to look interested. On two occasions, Rishaan even found her fiddling with her phone. By the time Rishaan was done, he knew exactly what he could expect from her.

'Super! It's a damn good script. I loved the hero's character,' she beamed effusively.

'Do you think I should tone down the political bit? Will it alienate the younger audience?'

Kiara wasn't sure.

'No. Why should it? It seems fine to me,' she said diffidently.

A moment later, Kiara added that she was probably not the best person to give him the right feedback.

As they drove back in the wee hours of morning, Kiara could sense Rishaan's nervousness. She, for the first time, felt a bit guilty for not being there for Rishaan, as much as she would have wanted to. She rested her head on his shoulder and said, 'Don't worry. Your efforts will bear fruit.'

♦

A few hours later, Kiara and Rishaan threw their first house-party to celebrate what seemed like Rishaan's first major breakthrough in his scripting career: Aakash Jha had simply loved Rishaan's script. And Rishaan, along with Jha, was going to narrate it next week to the hero, Ravi Dewan. Once Ravi gave his nod, Rishaan would be signed on as the writer. Given Ravi's proximity to Jha and the fact that the actor–director duo had done six movies together, Ravi's okay seemed a mere formality. Rishaan would get a sum of ₹15 lacs for the story and screenplay, 25 per cent of which would be given to him immediately upon signing. For Rishaan, it was a huge relief. He had not mentioned this to Kiara, but he wasn't in the best financial state. If not for this deal, he would have had to break a fixed deposit of his to cough up the next month's rent. He was glad he did not have to do that anymore.

In the past three hours that Rishaan was away from home, Kiara had immersed herself in Buddhist chants to invoke all the luck in the world for her man. She, of course, didn't say this to him. On returning, Rishaan had spontaneously hugged and kissed her with not a murmur escaping his mouth. She simply sensed he had good news for her.

It was Kiara's initiative to throw a party and celebrate Rishaan's big success. She immediately called up five of Rishaan's buddies and four of hers and an exciting agenda were set for the Saturday night. Between the arrangements, Rishaan slipped in his wish to visit the Siddhivinayak Temple on the coming Tuesday evening to offer prayers. Kiara happily agreed to accompany him.

It had been long since Rishaan had thrown a party at his place. His apartment buzzed with activity as loud music blazed across the living room. Kiara had arranged for the drinks, while Rishaan had himself cooked Mutton Biryani for the guests. A cook was arranged to come and fry the starters.

Hence, at an economical budget they seemed to have managed a rather lavish house party.

Rishaan's friends, who were invited for the party, included Mohit, an actor who had played the lead in a couple of serials, Ujjwal, his schoolmate from Lucknow, and his ex-colleagues from Star, Karan and Rashi. Kiara's friends included Jyoti, Simran, Amit and Ranbir, who were all her batchmates from her MBA days.

Except for Ranbir and Simran, who were seeing each other, the rest were all single. Rishaan's friend Mohit was known to be brazenly flirtatious, while Kiara's friend Jyoti was this starry-eyed babe who seemed to be in awe of anybody whom she had seen on TV. It was not a wonder, then, that Mohit and Jyoti seemed to hit it off particularly well. Star-struck, Jyoti kept asking Mohit details about his profession, his work schedule and his fitness regime.

A couple of drinks down, the conversation veered towards Mohit's personal life. Jyoti was very curious to know if Mohit was really having an affair with his co-star as reported in the media. Mohit was only too happy to play ball. He went into one of the bedrooms on the pretext of a smoke, with Jyoti following close behind him.

Kiara and Rishaan were elated to see their guests gel well with each other. Soon, the gathering broke into smaller groups with Rishaan interacting more with Kiara's friends and Kiara with his. As the effects of intoxication began to show, conversations became more animated. Everything seemed hunky-dory and well, until a loud shriek from the bedroom put the chitter-chatter to a sudden eerie pause.

'Dare you touch me, Mohit? How sick can you be?' Jyoti

yelled, as others entered the room.

Kiara and Rishaan were shocked to learn that Mohit had tried acting fresh with Jyoti and despite her warding him off, had tried smooching her.

'All you bloody actors are like this. The moment you find someone praising you, you think you can bed her. Disgusting!'

Mohit finally hit back.

'And you girls are bloody hypocrites. You flirt, you tell us suggestive things and then we get tempted, you put on this touch-me-not pretence. What the hell? Didn't you want us to sneak inside, alone and away from others?'

Rishaan and Kiara were both confused. Jyoti was completely sloshed, which didn't make her case any better. She soon broke down.

Seeing Jyoti break down, Kiara demanded that Mohit apologize to her.

'That's no way to talk to a woman,' she snubbed Mohit.

Rishaan, on the other hand, wasn't sure if it was Mohit's fault.

'Listen Kiara, I have known Mohit for three years and I know that he doesn't cross his limits. I don't think we should be judgmental.'

To this, Kiara shot back rather angrily.

'What are you trying to say Rishaan? Just because a girl hits it off well with him, he thinks he can sleep with her?'

'No, I am not saying that. But are you sure the girl did not give confusing signals herself?'

'That's the problem with you guys. The moment a girl opens up a bit with you, you think she is available.'

Rishaan's remark embarrassed Jyoti and she began crying even louder.

This led to Kiara's friend, Ranbir, and Rishaan's friend, Rashi, joining the argument. Ranbir said he had seen Mohit hitting on Jyoti rather brazenly. Rashi countered it by questioning if Jyoti was a kid to not realize it. 'I mean, I would hold myself guilty, if I lead a guy up to this sort of behaviour,' she reasoned.

Seeing the situation worsen, Rishaan's other friend, Karan, tried to intervene. He requested Mohit to apologize for the sake of peace. Mohit, instead, left the party abruptly. This led to a rather ugly altercation between Rishaan and Kiara with Rishaan accusing her of insulting his friend. Kiara told him to accept that what his friend did was wrong. With the guests around, they didn't prolong the argument. But by then, the camaraderie had long soured. Soon after, the guests left one by one and the party ended on a rather unpleasant note.

That night, Rishaan and Kiara had an extended skirmish with each finding faults with the other's attitude. Rishaan accused 'women like Kiara' of being 'fake feminists', while Kiara accused 'men like Rishaan' of being 'brazen chauvinists'. The argument turned rather nasty when Rishaan told her, 'You don't need to showcase your liberal self by dressing up scantily in front of the delivery boys and watchmen.' Kiara hit back by telling him, 'Men like you are plain hypocrites. You make passes at every scantily-clad woman, but if they fall in love with you, you then expect her to be covered from head till toe.'

Rishaan labelled her 'sick', and walked out of the room. Rishaan found it very disturbing that Kiara never understood his point. Not because she didn't want to but because she was too full of herself. Kiara hated the fact that the guy she intended to marry wasn't quite able to accept a woman the way she was. Why did he always have an opinion on the way a woman should be?

Given that the comments from both sides were rather acerbic, a certain bitterness in the air was inevitable. That night, Kiara and Rishaan slept in separate rooms!

The next morning, Rishaan's maid bunked the duty. As Kiara remained asleep till 11, Rishaan prepared pasta for breakfast and ate it all. When Kiara woke up, she was peeved for find none left for her.

'How selfish is that, Rishaan?' she charged at him. Rishaan continued to watch the cricket match on TV, unperturbed.

When Kiara repeated the word 'selfish', it had Rishaan blow a fuse.

'Oh! Wow! I am selfish, is it? Till date, have you ever offered me a cup of tea by yourself? On your birthday, you did not take out time for me. You hardly take any interest in what I do. Your friends are the most pious people on earth while mine are all perverts, right? You have no control over your drinking or smoking habits. And on top of that, you have the audacity to call me selfish?'

The impact of Rishaan's outburst was rather devastating. Kiara felt extremely hurt to hear his grouses. Unwilling to play the ball, she quickly got herself ready and left the house in a fit of anger.

'Where are you going?' Rishaan asked.

'Why do you want to know?'

Kiara spent the day watching a movie, all alone, in the

theatre and then spent a couple of hours at the Juhu beach gazing into the sea. She had done this before, twice actually, when she needed to put her thoughts into perspective.

For the next two days, conversations between Rishaan and Kiara were minimal. Rishaan spent most of his time watching movies at home. He needed the visual escape to keep his nerves intact.

On Tuesday night, it was already 10.30 p.m. and Kiara had still not returned home. Rishaan grew a bit worried. He tried calling her but her cell was switched off. Rishaan enquired from one of her colleague if she knew about Kiara's whereabouts. The colleague informed Rishaan that she and Kiara were in a meeting together at Star's Worli office, but the meeting had ended at 8 p.m. Post that, she had no clue where Kiara was.

Rishaan had begun the day reading about a gang-rape in the heart of the city. With Kiara not reachable at all, it was only natural for all sorts of negative thoughts to enter his mind. He started dialling her number frantically, hoping against odds a miracle would happen and the phone would connect. When he did not succeed, he set himself a target: at 11.30 p.m., he would go to the police station and register a complaint about not being able to locate her.

Soon time ran out. With some of the worst fears in mind, Rishaan stepped out of his house in search of Kiara. He pressed the lift button. Every second that lift took to arrive on his floor had his heart palpitate rather violently. Finally, the lift opened. And out came Kiara. She looked exhausted, but calm. She had a 'tika' on her forehead and carried a small basket in one hand with sweets, a broken coconut and a few flower petals.

Seeing Rishaan this hassled, she thus explained the situation.

'I completely forgot that we were supposed to go the Siddhivinayank Temple today. I remembered it around 8 p.m. when I was coming out from a meeting at Worli. It would not have been possible to call you there at such a short notice. Hence, on my way back, I visited the temple and offered prayers on behalf of both of us. Since it is Tuesday, the temple was very crowded, and so it took time to reach home. It was sheer bad luck that my cellphone, due to low-battery, had to conk off today.'

Tears welled up in Rishaan's eyes and he found it hard to contain them as he hugged her tight. He was rather touched by the fact that Kiara, who never enthused over the idea of idol worship, had travelled to the temple to do his bidding.

That night, after Kiara fell asleep, Rishaan, for the first time, explored something he had never done before. He chanted, *Nam Myoho Renge Kyo,* which Kiara would do when she'd be tense. While performing the chants, he kept wondering if he would ever be able to decipher Kiara in her entirety.

Ten

*There comes a time in every relationship
when you realize that love just isn't enough.*

Even as Rishaan and Kiara came to terms with their increased temperamental conflict, they were also pretty much aware of the fact that there were an equal number of factors, if not more, that were cementing their bond. Hence, it was sort of a happy situation, especially as these were still the early days of their relationship. In the last four months, they had experienced that which a normal couple would perhaps in say two years.

Kiara, for the first time, bought a couple of cooking books online, which she read in office whenever she found some free time. A few days later, on a Sunday morning, she got up early and prepared an Italian menu for breakfast: lasagne with three different types of cheese and some exotic sausage. To her surprise, she actually got the menu right and when she tasted it, it was incredibly yummy. Kiara was ecstatic; she had actually managed to cook all by herself.

Kiara had been discreet about her cooking experiments.

She had ensured that the ingredients were purchased while Rishaan was away for a meeting. Hence, he had no idea about it. When Rishaan sauntered into the kitchen at around 9 in the morning, he was livid to find that the maid had bunked the day again. And he was equally upset that Kiara ordered 'Italian' food every time the maid bunked.

'Come on, yaar. I would have prepared the breakfast,' he complained.

'So what's wrong if I did it?' asked Kiara calmly, already gorging on the food.

'You prepared this?' Rishaan muttered, disbelievingly rubbing his eyes.

It was the best lasagne that Rishaan had ever had in his life. And when he learnt of Kiara's efforts in learning to cook, he was simply astonished. Sunday had not seemed this homely in a very long time!

After breakfast, Rishaan called up his parents in Lucknow to have a longish chat which he usually reserved for Sunday mornings. Given his closeness with Mom, he confessed about living in with Kiara.

'So, we assume you will marry her?' his mom asked.

'I assume so too, Mom.'

It is strange that whenever Rishaan spoke about his future with Kiara, his words did not carry the same conviction as her's. He had stopped bothering himself about it, though, by believing that he was generally a bit more self-doubting than Kiara. Rishaan was delighted to learn that his mom would be coming down to Mumbai soon for a two-day teachers' conference, organized by a private company that specialized in designing educational softwares.

'Super, I am looking forward to making you meet Kiara,' he told Mom, before ending the conversation.

Rishaan went into the other bedroom to tell Kiara about this development. As he entered the room, Kiara who was discreetly checking something on the internet, turned towards him rather nervously.

'What happened?'

'N...no...nothing.'

He looked into the laptop screen and was quite stunned to see the page she was on. Babycenter.in!!! The heading read, 'Early Symptoms of Pregnancy'. He stared into Kiara's eyes and could see dread in them.

'Rishaan, I am worried I could be carrying... My period has been due since a week. I feel bloated and get tired easily. I don't know.'

She hugged Rishaan. A myriad emotions floated in his mind.

'Kiara, just chill. What if you are pregnant? So what? We could get married in the temple as early as next week.'

'Are you kidding?' she said in disbelief.

'Why? What's the big deal? I hate the idea of abortion.'

'Is everything that casual for you, Rishaan? Even I hate the thought of abortion. But pregnancy and childbirth are somethings I really want to plan. I don't want the most beautiful experience of my life to be an accident.'

Kiara did a home pregnancy test that evening. Even though the result showed negative, it hardly allayed her fears or anxieties. These anxieties persisted for the next three days and Rishaan had little idea of how to behave in such situations, apart from, showing empathy in abundance. He was largely aloof about the gravity of the situation. It was only three nights later when Kiara got her period that she finally heaved a sigh of relief. Rishaan was seated in a pub with a director-friend of his when he got her message, *Yipeee!! Got my period.* Rishaan wrote back, *Enjoy it.*

◆

Two days later, Rishaan suffered a setback when actor Ravi Dewan rejected his script. After sitting through Rishaan's narration for almost an hour, in which he kept fiddling with his cellphone most of the time, he finally gave the weirdest of reasons to back out.

'You know what, I have been doing similar movies with Jha. This time I want to do a mindless comedy.'

It was well known to Dewan that Jha would not come to him with a 'mindless comedy'. There was no point in keeping them on hold for the last few weeks. But then, given the massive clout that stars command in Bollywood, Jha showed absolutely no disappointment. Dewan and Jha, in fact, hugged each other and promised to work together in future, completely oblivious and ignorant of what Rishaan was going through.

As Jha and Rishaan drove back to the director's office, Jha could no longer hold his anger and unleashed some of the choicest invectives for Dewan.

'The ungrateful bastard is on cloud nine these days. I gave him his three biggest hits. Just wait and watch how he comes back to me after a year,' Jha cribbed.

For Rishaan, apart from the personal disappointment, he was beginning to hate the hypocrisy inherent in almost every top actor and director. For Rishaan, the setback was quite a big one. After his narration to Jha ten days ago, he was extremely confident that the signing amount of ₹3.75 lakhs was on its way. He was broken.

Upon returning home, Rishaan quickly checked his two bank accounts. There was hardly enough balance to pay the month's rent, which was due next week. The only way he could pay the rent was either by breaking a fixed deposit worth ₹2.25 lakhs or borrowing money from Kiara. He could not comprehend whether it was his chauvinist streak or some other factor, but borrowing from Kiara was instantly ruled out.

For the next couple of hours, he switched off the lights, lay on bed and did nothing. Grotesque thoughts about all that was happening in his life, tortured in his mind.

Suddenly, the doorbell rang. Kiara was standing in front of him, super excited, holding a cake in her hand. She was that confident about Ravi Dewan giving his nod.

'It's not happening,' said Rishaan in a heavy tone.

Rishaan was just too depressed to say anything. She hugged him; and conversation between them remained sparse.

Post dinner, Rishaan sat by the window wall all alone and looked out into the night as the fresh night breeze blew across. Sensing that he needed support, Kiara walked up to him and sat by his side.

'I know what you must be feeling,' said she, holding his hand. 'I know how much you had put into it.'

Rishaan seemed too depressed to chat.

'Have you thought of a Plan B?' Kiara asked him.

'What plan B?'

'Would you like to get back to a regular job, maybe in a consultant's profile? Something that offers you flexible timings.'

This unsuspecting suggestion from Kiara had Rishaan flare up.

'Is that the level of confidence you have in me? Just one setback and you don't have the patience to let me pursue what I want to do?' he snubbed her.

'Of course not, Rishaan. I just thought that if you have an option, the next setback will not make you feel as depressed as you are now,' Kiara explained herself, quite taken aback by his sharp reaction.

'I am alright, Kiara. I can't let this failure get the better of me. Don't worry about me.'

Rishaan went off in a huff and watched television till the wee hours of the morning. As Kiara lay on bed, she couldn't escape thinking how a rather harmless suggestion from her had triggered such a sharp reaction from Rishaan. Were they so different in the way they perceived situations? Or, was it a case of Rishaan's inflated ego? If it was the latter, she might just have to brace herself for some more fireworks in future.

Relationships are complex; and every passing day was only reiterating this upon Rishaan and Kiara.

Eleven

> *To love is nothing. To be loved is something.*
> *But to love and be loved, that's everything.*
> —T. TOLIS

Rishaan's mom had to attend a two-day seminar on 'Changing Perspectives of School Education' in Mumbai, which fell on Friday and Saturday. The seminar was at Churchgate, almost at the opposite end of the town where Rishaan lived. She had planned to visit Rishaan on the Saturday evening, after the seminar was over, and stay back till late Sunday. But, it so happened that the organizers had arranged for a surprise after seminar dinner. And this last minute change-of-plan had the Mom visit Rishaan on Friday evening itself. Since she was well aware of Rishaan's everyday schedule, therefore instead of informing him beforehand, she decided to give him a surprise. At around quarter to seven, the doorbell rang; Rishaan thinking it to be Kiara since she had an office party later that evening and was supposed to return home early. Rishaan was shocked to find his mom standing at his doorstep. He quickly bent to touch her feet and ushered her inside.

The house was in a complete mess. Rishaan's mom had always chided him for not keeping his stuff in place. But now that there was a girl in the house, she was hoping that things might have improved. Well, the truth was, the place looked more haphazard than before.

'Hmm...It seems you've found someone exactly like yourself,' she said jocularly, upon entering the house.

Rishaan prepared tea for Mom and then both sat down to chat. Mom and son were meeting after six months. Had it not been for her official trip, their meeting would have taken place only around Diwali. He informed her about the recent rejection with regards to the film script he had written for director Aakash Jha. It was only three days ago that the possibility of becoming a scriptwriter in Bollywood had seemed so certain. Upon sensing that her son was still recovering from the dejection, she shifted the conversation to his personal life.

'So tell me more about Kiara?'

'Hmm...She's difficult to describe.'

The matter-of-fact answer left Rishaan's mom a bit surprised.

'In fact, she'll be in any moment. Why don't you just meet her and see yourself? I think that should be more fun. I haven't told her much about you either.'

'Yes, that should be interesting. But at least tell me how long have you known her?'

'Four months.'

'And for how long have you guys been living together?'

'Two months.'

Rishaan's mom tried her best not to sound opinionated

about the situation, yet her concern for Rishaan was only too visible on her face.

When Kiara did not return by 7.30 p.m., Rishaan called to know her whereabouts and inform her about his mom's early arrival. She was stuck in a traffic jam and couldn't hear him properly. Since the cellphone signal was particularly bad, all Kiara could hear was the word 'mom' and nothing more. Sensing the urgency in his voice, she informed him of being stuck in a traffic jam and that she would reach home in 15 minutes, when suddenly the phone got disconnected.

'Actually Kiara had to attend an office party tonight. But now she won't go,' Rishaan informed his mom in passing, presuming Kiara's decision would be same.

'Oh, in that case, I should not have come today,' said his mom.

'No, no, Mom. You did the right thing by surprising me.'

She relaxed on the couch for some time and then excused herself to go to the washroom and freshen up. When she came out some minutes later, she seemed rather shocked.

'Come here Rishaan,' she said, leading him to the washroom.

Rishaan went in to see what was amiss. On the ventilator's window pane there lay two cigarette stubs.

'When did you start smoking son? I have only seen you detest cigarette smoke,' she said, confused.

The query left Rishaan utterly embarrassed.

'Oh Mom, I smoke very occasionally. Only when I feel stressed or restless. You know freelancing can get a bit tough at times,' he smiled sheepishly, struggling for an explanation.

For the next ten minutes, Mom counselled Rishaan on

ways to beat stress by practising yoga and meditation for just half an hour daily. Rishaan had started to hate Kiara for landing him in such an embarrassing situation, when the doorbell rang.

It was Kiara. She had reached home looking all hassled and cribbing about the traffic. When she saw Rishaan's mom, for a moment she didn't know how to react. Rishaan gestured to touch the Mom's feet, which she immediately obliged to do. After indulging in some basic sweet talk with his mother, Kiara finally managed to grab a private moment with Rishaan.

'I have to go for my office party,' she told Rishaan.

'Oh come on Kiara, you can bunk tonight's party.'

'Rishaan, I would have, if I had known aunty was coming. But now everybody is expecting me to be there. Besides, my boss has thrown this party to celebrate his promotion. If I skip it, it will leave a very bad impression.'

Rishaan, who was already annoyed with Kiara for leaving those cigarette stubs on the washroom window, quite hated it when she appeared this selfish. But then, he did not want to create a scene in front of Mom, and so decided to let go.

'Can I at least expect you to come back early?'

'Surely. I can do that.'

'In that case, Mom and I will have dinner outside and then the three of us could drive down town to drop Mom to her hotel.'

'That sounds good.'

'Let me also inform you beforehand that Mom will be coming home again on this Sunday morning, to have lunch with us before flying back to Lucknow.'

The formal and assertive tone in which Rishaan divulged

the information made it pretty apparent that he wanted to tell Kiara in no certain terms: 'You better not mess up again on Sunday.'

Kiara did not like Rishaan's tone, but she understood that Rishaan had reasons to be upset as much as she had reasons to do what she was doing. She quickly got around to taking a shower and got ready for the party. Even as Rishaan chatted with his mom, he was clearly feeling let down by Kiara. His mom, being his mom, knew exactly what was upsetting him.

As Rishaan and his mom chatted in the living room, Kiara came out all dressed to leave for the party. She was wearing a short black dress that covered her only till her thighs. Rishaan looked at her disapprovingly as she made her way to where they were sitting. She then spent some five minutes with Rishaan's mom, trying to make sweet talk. But the more she tried, the more obvious things became, impending a natural chemistry.

And soon it was time to leave for the party. Her colleague had arrived and was waiting for her outside the building. Kiara bid farewell to Rishaan and his mother and had almost exited the house when she realized that she might have forgotten to take the house keys. Already late for the party, Kiara frantically searched her purse. She found the house keys but not before something else fell out of her bag: the cigarette lighter.

Both Rishaan and Kiara were utterly embarrassed in front of Mom. Kiara quickly picked up the lighter, and knowing that she had goofed up big time, sheepishly excused herself. On the other hand, Rishaan's mom had a look of vindication on her face, 'I was right. Rishaan could not have taken to smoking.' Looking at his son, who was red with embarrassment, Mom skilfully changed the topic, 'Where do you want to go for dinner?'

♦

That evening when Rishaan and his mom sat over dinner at a rooftop restaurant in Andheri, long pauses impeded the natural flow of their conversation. Rishaan, who was feeling very low, ended up discussing his confusion about Kiara—the fact that he sometimes found her too selfish and aloof, and yet she was the one more confident and vocal about spending her entire life with him than he was with her. As they got talking, Rishaan told his mom about her traumatic past. He wasn't sure if telling her was the right thing to do though. But then these thoughts and confusion needed an outlet. On the contrary, his mom absorbed it all without being judgmental.

'Do you love her?' she asked him directly.

Thrice Rishaan tried answering it, yet, for want of clarity, held his words back.

'I think I need a little more time to figure out the answer,' he replied finally.

'Take your time, son. But make sure you are absolutely convinced about the decision you take. It's a decision that will impact your life ahead,' she advised.

That night when Kiara did not call from the party, Rishaan chose to ignore her. He instead drove his mom back to the hotel alone. There was an uneasy silence between mom and son. Mom had been far too gracious to not have said anything against Kiara. But then neither did she say anything that would have hinted at her acceptance for Kiara. Rishaan was quite close to his mom, and a sense that she was not happy about any of his choices was enough to leave him doubting about it forever. Rishaan's mom, for her part, had never imposed her decision on her son. After dropping her to the hotel, the journey back home seemed lonelier than ever to him.

◆

On Saturday, Rishaan and Kiara didn't talk much. Kiara was certainly apologetic about her not being able to give time to Rishaan's mom. But that's all she was. Rishaan was doubtful whether she was genuinely sorry, but wanted to avoid an argument early in the day. In some time, he left for the bank. Kiara too spent the afternoon in the parlour, thinking how she could mend the situation. And so before they hit the bed at night, Kiara apologized again and promised to prepare the Sunday lunch all by herself for Mom.

Sunday had arrived. Rishaan's mom called him early in the morning and requested the two to come down to the Siddhivinayank Temple to offer prayers together. Kiara, who had already begun making arrangements for the lunch requested to be left out.

Even as Rishaan's mom prayed at the Siddhivinayak Temple for her son's happiness, Rishaan watched her devotion with mixed feelings. When they reached home, Rishaan was quite upbeat about Kiara winning over his mom with a stellar performance. Instead, Rishaan was in for a big shock. Kiara was almost in tears: the *mutter paneer* she had prepared was burnt and tasteless while the *pulao* was just about okay. Kiara was extremely upset and apologetic for the lapse. When Rishaan asked her how it all happened, she blamed it on an urgent phone call.

'Wow! So this is what you skipped the temple visit for,' Rishaan taunted her, annoyed.

'Don't be sarcastic, Rishaan. You know how miserable I am feeling right now.'

Rishaan had just about managed his anger, but an undercurrent of tension prevailed throughout the day.

That evening after Rishaan's mom left for Lucknow, Rishaan decided to have a chat with Kiara. There were far too many things about her attitude that had begun to bother him and he needed to discuss them with her. Kiara was as upset about what had transpired in the last two days but wanted to avoid talking about it. That evening when Kiara went to the washroom, Rishaan did something he had never done before: he checked her cellphone for call records. To his shock, there were 5 missed calls from Ajit between 10 and 11 in the morning and then at 11.17, she had called Ajit and the conversation had gone on for 32 minutes. So this is what led the *mutter paneer* to burn? Rishaan stood livid thinking about it.

When Kiara came out, Rishaan was still holding her cellphone.

'Why did you have to call Ajit for 32 minutes in the middle of cooking?' he demanded to know.

'Well, you know Ajit had been calling me for the last two days. He's found a girlfriend on his Europe trip, a Russian girl who was also on a holiday. Both of them believe that they're madly in love. And you know what, both of them want to go by their instincts and get married as early as possible. Isn't that amazing? I mean, how love just happens to people,' Kiara explained, unable to hold back her excitement.

Rishaan remained unmoved, looking straight into her eyes in an intense, questioning way. Sensing his anger, Kiara went and held him from behind in a comforting manner.

'I am sorry, darling. I am really sorry.'

At this point, Rishaan suddenly burst out in a way Kiara had never seen him before, his decibel levels rising to atrocious levels.

'What all will you be sorry for Kiara? What all, tell me?' he roared.

'What do you mean?'

'You cannot give up smoking. Forget office meetings, even an office party is more important for you than spending time with my mother. Did you have to wear that short black dress in front of her? On top of it, you spoil the dish you were preparing for her because you were talking to your ex?'

For a moment, Kiara was shaken by the intensity of his protest. Did Rishaan really have so many issues with her? If yes, then had they been living in denial so far? Given the foul mood that Rishaan was in, Kiara chose not to prolong the debate.

'Listen Rishaan, I am really sorry. I just smoke one or two cigarettes now, that too only to beat the pangs of restlessness I sometimes feel. As for the short black dress, that's the way I usually dress up for parties. If aunty did not like me wearing it, you should have told me beforehand.'

'What all do you expect me to spoon feed you, Kiara? It's not about Mom liking something or not. It's about you realizing how you need to come in front of people, be it a grocery delivery boy or my mom. It's about you, damn it.'

Rishaan's last sentence sounded like an assault on her

very identity. It devastated her. She took a moment to gather herself before answering.

'Rishaan, is there anything that you like in me?'

Rishaan fumbled for an answer, when he said, 'Your... your honesty.'

Kiara, who was by now seething in anger, shot back.

'You're lying, Rishaan. You like nothing about me. Have you ever tried to accept me the way I am? I never tell you how to dress or who should be your friends or persuade you to do the Buddhist chants. But you simply have a tendency to impose things on me.'

'Kiara, don't confuse issues. If there were certain lapses in your behaviour, its better you accept it.'

'Fair enough, I accept it. Tell me what you like about me apart from my honesty?'

Rishaan had no answer.

'Good sex?'

This pointed query put Rishaan in a rather uncomfortable situation.

'I am asking you Rishaan, I need to know. What binds us, apart from good sex? Is there nothing else?'

Seeing Kiara get hysterical, Rishaan really did not know what to say.

'You know what Rishaan, the way you boss around me at times, without ever trying to understand me, it sometimes make me feel that you treat me like a whore.'

When he heard this, Rishaan could not hold himself back anymore and impulsively raised his hand in a fit of rage and stopped right in front of her face.

'Hit me, Rishaan. Come on, hit me. Why did you stop?

Isn't that what most men think is their birth right?'

Rishaan calmed down with great difficulty, before giving it back to her.

'You know what the problem with women like you is? You take the word "liberated" far too seriously. You do not know what to say when, what to wear where, and simply believe that men are idiots. With this kind of an attitude, I am not sure we can go very far. Our future together is doomed.'

Rishaan walked off to the other room and banged the door behind him. Kiara broke down into uncontrollable tears. An hour later, despite Rishaan's countless apologies, she packed her bag and left the house. She shifted to her colleague Kajal's house, who stayed close by at the Yari Road.

It was a long, sleepless night for both Rishaan and Kiara. The journey of the last four months suddenly seemed to have come to a naught. Were the last four months an illusion? How unpredictable could life and relationships be?

As Rishaan and Kiara restlessly turned on their bed all night, they probably missed each other as much as they felt betrayed. The last four months had been magically blissful. Was the magic over? Or was there still a way it could be salvaged?

Past imperfect, future tense is what aptly described the point at which Rishaan and Kiara found themselves in that long endless night.

Twelve

> If I know what love is, it is because of you.
> —HERMAN HESSE

March 2014

Two weeks had passed since Rishaan and Kiara returned from their baby-making trip to Goa. And now it was that time of the month most couples trying to conceive excitedly wait for and those, who had been trying for far too long look forward to dreadfully.

With Kiara's period overdue by two days, it was time to take the home pregnancy test. On Friday, when Rishaan dropped Kiara to her office, he said to her, 'Just be calm, Kiara. I know it is round the corner. I have a hunch you are pregnant this time.' They decided to take the test in the evening, after Kiara returned from work.

At 4 in the evening, Rishaan got a call from Kiara. He picked it up wondering if there was any good news: either she'd have gotten her period or she must have experienced some pregnancy symptom.

'Ye...ah, Kirara,' he said tentatively.

Kiara, who was calling from inside her office washroom, broke down on the phone. She wept inconsolably like a child as she was bleeding profusely.

Rishaan and Kiara spent the weekend mulling over their repeated disappointments in the last one year. They were left with only two options: either to continue trying, which would only make them more miserable if success continued to elude them like it had so far; or to seriously consider and opt for alternatives such as the IVF (In Vitro Fertilization). Rishaan left the final decision on Kiara. It was she who wanted a baby desperately and hence, it made sense to let her take the call. By Sunday night, Kiara had made up her mind: she would much rather make things happen than continue to suffer by hopelessly hoping for a miracle.

Rishaan sought an appointment with a leading infertility specialist in Bandra, Dr Shah. They got one for Wednesday afternoon. Kiara bunked office on Wednesday while Rishaan kept himself free to keep their appointment with the doctor.

Dr Shah, a suave gentleman in his mid-forties, who claimed to have helped more than a thousand women conceive via IVF, had a word of caution for them, 'The success rate of IVF is only around 20 per cent, which is as good as trying normally, provided, of course, there is no other anomaly. So please be prepared for a possible situation where the IVF doesn't bear fruit.'

'Doctor, I...I mean we have made up our minds. We want to go for it,' Kiara asserted.

'Great! You know what; faith in the Almighty often succeeds where medical science fails. You will require lots of patience and luck in the weeks ahead,' the good-natured doctor advised.

Kiara had to go through a set of advanced hormonal tests before the IVF process was set in motion. The journey to the doctor's clinic and back home was rather unnerving. It somehow made Kiara feel quite inadequate, when she knew she wasn't. Rishaan, on the other hand, managed to treat the situation more clinically, not letting it affect his psyche.

As the two entered home, Kiara could not hold back her tears anymore. The times were tough and the two needed to be strong. She broke down and wept inconsolably for the next half an hour. It took a mammoth effort on Rishaan's part to calm her down

Rishaan prepared tea and sandwiches for her. They had them sitting on the bed. When Kiara seemed more in control, Rishaan rested his head on her lap, as Kiara caressed his forehead and gently ran her fingers through his hair.

'Don't lose hope, Kiara. Trust me, my mental state is no better than yours. Optimism is all that keeps me going. I just cannot afford to be pessimistic...not for both of us,' he told her.

Probably realizing that she was being unfair to Rishaan, Kiara decided to shun despondency. She conjured a brave façade and changed the topic of discussion. For the rest of the evening, they avoided talking about the issue at hand. Instead, they sought escape in an old seventies potboiler, *Amar Akbar Antony*, which they saw on a DVD. By dinner time, Rishaan and Kiara were in a much better mood. Rishaan took her out for dinner to a Chinese restaurant close by and by the time they returned, they were already more confident to cope with the pressure months ahead of them.

Rishaan and Kiara hit the bed to end what had been a

really long day. And as customary, Rishaan quickly switched on the TV to surf the latest news. In front of them, on the television, flashed the Breaking News, almost in all the channels: indiscriminate firing of bullets by an unknown assassin at a kids' school in a small town called Bradford, near New York, had killed more than twenty-five children and a teacher, and critically injured another lady teacher.

Rishaan switched off the television immediately, knowing very well of the emotional hardships they were anyway going through. He put Kiara to sleep and battled with his thoughts for some time before taking refuge in slumber.

At 2.45 a.m., while the two were fast asleep, Rishaan's cell phone rang. It was an international number, most probably from the USA, he deduced. Not recognizing the number, he didn't take the call. A moment later, Kiara's phone started ringing as well. She looked at her cellphone and was surprised to find two missed calls from the same international number. They wondered who could be trying to reach them at that odd an hour. In the next two minutes, Rishaan's cell phone rang again. This time, he hurriedly pressed the answering button.

'Rishaan Kumar?' queried an old man in an American accent.

'Yes.' Rishaan replied tentatively.

'This is Ian Robinson from Bradford, New York. Diya Kohli has been staying as my paying guest for the last two years. I have some bad news for you. Diya was a victim of today's gunfire at the Columbus school. She is critically injured and battling for her life at the Clinton Hospital here. Her personal diary had your number, and by gestures and written instructions she asked me to call you or your wife and inform about her condition.'

The caller took a couple of minutes to explain the situation. Once the conversation was over, an uncomfortable, unnerving silence descended upon the couple.

'Diya Kohli! She has been staying in Florida?' Kiara muttered to herself.

Rishaan, for his part, did not know how to react to the news; he could not figure out why of all people were they the first ones to get this news. Odd as it was, their behaviour gave an eerie feeling that perhaps some deep dark secret was lurking between them. For nearly half an hour, a confused silence persisted in the room, with both Rishaan and Kiara looking lost in thought.

'I think you should go to Florida,' Kiara said, finally after a long pause. 'Diya might be in need of urgent help.'

For a while, Rishaan did not respond as a gamut of thoughts and emotions flooded his mind.

'Are you sure that I should go? he finally asked, looking genuinely confused and undecided.

Kiara hugged him tight, seeming weakened by the unending chaos in her life.

Her suggestion was prompted by the consideration that she had to be in office for the next two days when her global bosses would be visiting their Indian office; Rishaan, on the other hand, was in between projects and could afford a week away. The other worry was a financial one: the high costs of making a US trip at such short notice. But then, Diya was his wife's best friend; how could he put her life at risk!

◆

Twelve hours later, when Rishaan's Cathay Pacific flight took off from the Chhatrapati Shivaji International Airport in Mumbai, he felt an unusual dread lingering inside him. He dreaded facing Diya after such a long time, and especially in the situation he was going to meet her in.

As he shut his eyes to relax his troubled head, his memory went back to the time when he first met Diya, almost four years ago.

Thirteen

> *The greatest happiness of life is the conviction that we are loved;*
> *loved for ourselves, or rather, loved in spite of ourselves.*
> —VICTOR HUGO

June 2010

Sometimes, distance makes the heart grow fonder, and at other times, it makes reconciliation impossible. Rishaan and Kiara seemed to be experiencing the former. They missed each other, notwithstanding the unsavoury situation that had been created between them. The two, none the wiser, kept the act on.

Rishaan had already missed the monthly date for paying the house-rent. He was aware of the lapse but chose to ignore it till his well-off landlord reminded him. There was little option available but to break a two-year-old fixed deposit.

One night in his sleep, Rishaan was blabbering, 'Kiara, it has been such a long time since we made love. Why are you avoiding me?' When he woke up, he realized why making love to her could well be history. He had messaged her couple of times to ask if she was alright. But Kiara restrained herself from answering, albeit with a heavy heart. Rishaan's words, 'With this kind of an attitude, our future together is doomed,' ricocheted in her ears. It shook her self-confidence. 'Am I such a difficult partner to be with? Why can I never find love in those I love? For all the exterior façade of being emotionally strong, do I actually give in to people too easily?'

One day when things didn't seem particularly good for Kiara in office, as she sat alone having her lunch, Kiara sent a message to Rishaan, *Khana khaya?* Rishaan, who had already softened up a bit, wrote a longish reply futilely hoping that it would revive their communication. Kiara got busy in sorting out a crisis in office and never replied back. That evening while returning home, she stopped at the Barista, Versova, hoping to find Rishaan there. But that was not to be.

◆

In the film industry, things sometime suddenly turn around in the most dramatic and unexpected of ways. Rishaan experienced this when he suddenly got a call from director Aakash Jha, nearly two weeks after their script had been rejected by Dewan.

'Rishaan, I have some good news for you,' said he. 'I narrated your script to Asif Khan. He loved it and wants to do this movie with us ASAP.'

Rishaan wasn't sure how to react. Asif was a rising star, no doubt, but nowhere in the league of Ravi Dewan.

'But Aakashji, wouldn't that mean scaling down the project? I mean, Asif just has one hit film to his credit.'

'Don't worry, Rishaan. When I first worked with Ravi, he too was one-film old, that too a flop one. I turned him into a superstar. I can do the same with Asif. And the best thing is, I have Eros to put money on Asif.'

And so, Rishaan signed his first film that very evening. The signing amount he received was ₹1.5 lakhs, much less than what he was supposed to get previously. But then, it wasn't a bad start at all. He had, after all, signed his first film as a writer, that too with one of Bollywood's topmost director.

Rishaan was so tempted to call Kiara and give her the news first. But something held him back and instead called his parents in Lucknow.

'Kiara must be so happy,' his mom remarked.

'Y...yes, she is,' he replied tentatively.

That evening, which happened to be a Saturday, Rishaan was left all by himself, with nobody around to celebrate his success. His friends from Star were off on an offsite to Lonavala, while his actor friend was on a night shoot. At around 9, when the forlornness started to get onto him, he stepped out of the house with no clear idea of where he wanted to go.

Rishaan drove his car to the same Versova Barista and occupied a table in the open air space outside the glass wall. It was an eerie coincidence that Kiara was seated right across in the air-conditioned section inside. She was busy chatting with her friends, Anu and Rajan. It was only when he turned towards them that Rajan noticed him and nudged Kiara to look in his direction. The chance encounter, something that both Kiara and Rishaan had been silently hoping for, turned out to be a rather weird one, with the glass door and lots of awkwardness separating them.

Rishaan took a moment to decide what to do. And then

he walked inside and stood right in front of Kiara's table.

'Kiara, I have some good news for you,' said he. Kiara tended to remain indifferent, even as her friends looked on.

'I signed my first movie today. I even received the signing amount,' he informed excitedly.

Kiara's face lit up with relief instantly. 'Congrats, Rishaan! I am so happy for you,' she hugged him. In her heart of hearts she was still quite hurt, and not her usual self. While her friends excitedly enquired Rishaan about the project, she merely heard out the details like a mute spectator. Rishaan was quick to sense the awkwardness, and knew he'd have to speak to her in private.

'Kiara, could you please come out with me for a moment?' he implored.

Kiara did not respond.

Rishaan repeated the query, this time, more pointedly and when Kiara continued to ignore him, he held her hand and led her outside. To his surprise, Kiara did not resist or protest. She perhaps wanted to see in him a greater sense of ownership for their relationship, which this act of aggression coincidentally had in it in good measure. He directed Kiara to get inside his car. As Rishaan drove around the suburbs, a mild drizzle soothed what had been an irritably humid day. Taking the cue, Rishaan lowered the volume of CD player and initiated the talk.

'Kiara, I am sorry for the way I behaved the other day. I really felt bad about it.' Kiara looked at him expectantly.

'You know, in the last four and half months I have shared my life with you like never before. Today, when I finally achieved what I had been chasing all these months, I wanted you to be around to share my success. I feel miserable staying away from you,' Rishaan explained.

'Now aren't you being selfish, Rishaan? I mean, you wanted me to be with you because you were feeling lonely and miserable. Did you care for the way I have felt these past seven days? Do you have any idea about the way I have been giving in to you? Or do you think I am used to giving in with people?'

Kiara was hysterical and obviously very hurt, which made things more difficult for Rishaan. In chaotic moments like these, Rishaan found the city more claustrophobic than ever. Hence, on an impulse, he pressed on the accelerator of the car and zoomed off in a direction opposite to where they stayed.

'Rishaan, stop the car. Where are we going?' Kiara demanded to know.

He said nothing.

'Rishaan, stop it. I am not in the mood for a thoughtless outing.'

Driving his car at full speed on the Western Express Highway, he turned to her and kissed her passionately. Kiara realized that she was not strong enough to resist the indulgence and reciprocated with equal passion.

Two hours later, Rishaan and Kiara were at the virgin beach of Kihim, near Alibaug. As they sat in the car, they could hear the sea moving towards them and the waves crashing some 50 metres away from where they were parked. Sporadic streak of lightning lit the sky and the rain clouds thundered rather menacingly.

Rishaan and Kiara, seemed completely unaffected by the ominous weather outside. With a bottle of beer each in their hands and the car windows slid-open, they seemed to be at peace in each other's' company. Rishaan turned towards Kiara and saw her looking at him, rather lost and somewhat high.

The clouds roared again, this time even more menacingly. Rishaan rolled up the car windows, turned on the air-conditioner and played out some of the best Bryan Adams numbers. In this rather seemingly perfect ambience, they embraced each other and indulged themselves physically. In just over ten minutes, they made love, it being their most surreal experience due to the surrounding turbulence, both external and internal which they had been battling.

The consummation during the heavy showers made them wonder if the heavens were doling out their blessings on their reunion. They drove back to Mumbai amidst heavy rains. The two-hour journey back home took nearly seven hours, with multiple stopovers to escape the nature's fury. The time they spent together stuck in the rains, they arrived at an understanding of sorts: Rishaan would try and accept Kiara the way she was; Kiara, on the other hand, would try to spend more time with Rishaan and be more involved with his work.

Monsoon, the season Rishaan was craving for ever since it ended the previous year, had finally arrived and, that too, with a bang. Rishaan and Kiara were back to living together!

Two days later when a colleague of Kiara's, also her confidant, asked her about her relationship status, Kiara said, 'He is a difficult partner, yet one who is very addictive and difficult to live without.' On the other hand, Rishaan confided in his actor friend, 'Right now, I love her. But you know what, I think she has a bit of a rebellious, self-destructive tendency in her. As long as she does not do something that spoils the relationship, this one is for keeps.'

Rishaan, thus, quite unfairly, put the onus of sustaining the relationship on Kiara.

◆

Lately, Kiara had been talking about Rishaan to her mother, Janki. She had confided about their brief estrangement and then the patch-up. They had discussed Rishaan's temperamental behaviour, which Kiara felt was largely due to his uncertain career as an independent scriptwriter.

That weekend, Kiara's mom came over to Mumbai. She wanted to meet the guy her daughter was living with. Kiara's mom found Rishaan 'okay'. In the one day she spent with the two, there was nothing she particularly liked or disliked about him; which was understandable considering that Rishaan usually took his own time to open up in front of people.

Before Janki left for Delhi, she had an hour's chat with Kiara and Rishaan, and made her preferences known.

'I understand the stage you both are in. It's that stage where you believe in utopia. You believe in the illusion called perfection. And for no real reason, you tend to be overly finicky. But trust me, if you both had enough factors binding you together for five months, the same factors might suffice for the next forty years as well. It's all in the mind.'

Kiara and Rishaan heard Janki out, acknowledging the truth to be what she said.

'In my opinion, you should take a call very soon. Either get engaged and work towards marriage or break-up. Do not waste your time and emotions,' she said, rather unemotionally, her own experiences making her sound more cut and dry than she actually was.

After Rishaan and Kiara dropped Janki to the airport, they had a chat about what Janki had advised them.

'Rishaan, next Saturday is your birthday. Let's throw a party on Friday night for all our friends and make the announcement.'

'What announcement?' Rishaan asked, a bit confused.

'That we are getting engaged and will get married in a year's time.'

Rishaan nodded. He seemed fine with the first part, not so fine with the latter.

Rishaan had realized that he was pretty indecisive on personal matters. And so, he decided to go with the flow. He let Kiara decide the future for him. He had anyway never really fallen in love. And if he could not fall in love with Kiara even after living with her for so many months, then perhaps he was not cut out for love. He took a backseat and let Kiara plan and execute what promised to be his most fateful birthday party.

In the following five days leading to his birthday, Kiara worked out the party to its minutest details. She wanted it to be the best of Rishaan's twenty-five birthdays. And of course this one was special: it would mark the formal start of their life together. They were going public about their relationship.

The party was planned at a popular night spot in Juhu called Orris.

Just two nights before the party, when an exhausted Kiara was about to hit the bed, something unexpected happened. Kiara got a call from her best buddy Diya. To Kiara's shock, Diya was in the middle of a major crisis. She sounded choked and on the verge of breaking down.

'Kiara, I am coming back to India. I am landing on Friday night,' she informed.

'But what's the matter Diya? Are you alright?'

'I can't talk much on the phone right now except that it's all over between Derek and me. In fact something really obnoxious happened after which I can't stay with him for a single moment. I cannot tell you anything more on phone.'

'Diya, where will you be staying in Mumbai?'

'With my bua, in Chembur?'

'Have you informed her yet?'

'No. I am going to call her now. It all happened very suddenly.'

'Hmm.'

Knowing how mean Diya's bua was, Kiara persuaded and convinced Diya to stay with her in Mumbai. Diya agreed but only on the condition that within a month, she would find a job and move out. Rishaan overheard the entire conversation. He hated the fact that Kiara did not consider it important to check with him before inviting her friend to stay over at their place.

'Oh come on, Kiara. You should have at least checked with me,' he complained.

'What's there to check with you, Rishaan? If your best buddy was in such a crisis, would you not invite him to stay over at your place?' she shot back, before adding somewhat sarcastically, 'Oh I forgot that you don't have real buddies.'

'Listen Kiara. I am not saying not to help your friend. But please remember that I work out of home and I need peace to concentrate. I don't think either you or I have got the time to get sucked into other people's problems.'

'She is not other people, Rishaan. She is my best friend, she's a part of me.'

Kiara assured Rishaan that she would help Diya find an accommodation within a week, 'But right now Diya needs our support.'

◆

Diya's flight was scheduled to land in Mumbai at 10.15 p.m., which coincided with the party timings. It was decided that Kiara would hire a driver for that night. The driver would take Rishaan's car to the airport, pick Diya up and drop her home. She would anyway be jet-lagged and not in the right state to come to the party. Rishaan and Kiara would, in that case, wind up the party with the big announcement shortly after mid-night and get home to be with Diya.

Rishaan's birthday party didn't seem any different from the parties he had attended in Mumbai in the last three years. They were allotted one side of the disc floor, which could accommodate around forty people, for the party. With loud music blazing into their ears, something Rishaan detested, he could hardly make proper conversation with anyone. He wondered why Kiara had thrown such a wannabe party, when she knew he preferred quieter, open-air get-togethers. He remembered his promise to Kiara: to try and accept her the way she was. And after all, she had done as much as she could to make his birthday special. Why wasn't he happy then? Did he expect a bit too much from Kiara? Or had he already begun to take her for granted?

Considering it was a weekday, guests started pouring in

only around 10 and by 11 it was a packed house: nearly half of them Kiara's friends and the rest Rishaan's.

Rishaan stood in a corner accepting the greetings, quite unlike a birthday boy and clearly not at ease with the crowd around. Kiara, on the other hand, did what she enjoyed the most on such occasions: mingled with guests and effortlessly grooved to the music. She was conscious though of Rishaan's dislike for her getting drunk beyond tolerable limits. Hence, avoided liquor altogether.

Rishaan's tomboyish boss Mita, who was also invited to the party, had been observing him for a long time. Seeing him look utterly lost, she walked up to him for a quick chat. 'So what's the plan? Are you two getting married anytime soon?' Mita, who was already a bit tipsy, asked him.

'If it's destined, why not,' replied a rather preoccupied Rishaan.

At this point, Kiara came rushing to him. She pulled him aside and said, 'Darling, I have a small request. Please don't say no. My friends are insisting I have a drink with them. Just one peg. Will you allow me?'

Rishaan nodded.

With a glass of Vodka in her hand Kiara grooved passionately to the beats. In no time, two of her friends, both ostensibly in awe of her, joined her on the dance floor. This did not make for a very happy sight for Rishaan. But then, what was keeping him quiet? Why was he suddenly getting the vibes that he did not belong to the celebrations that had been planned for him? Rishaan continued chatting with Mita, while Mita couldn't help compare the current situation with the one a few months ago at the Star party, where Rishaan and Mita looked like they were yearning to be with each other. Did proximity create distance?

In the midst of all the celebration, what Kiara did not realize was that somebody she didn't want to see ever again was present at the same disc: Rahul Grover. Rahul was there with his friends, but his eyes were constantly glued on Kiara. When Kiara finally stepped out to visit the washroom, he stalked her to the washroom and was waiting outside for her to return. The moment Kiara stepped out, she chanced upon him and was stunned by this sudden encounter. Rahul sported a stubble, had put on weight and had not dyed his widely greying hair. All in all, he did not seem to be in great spirits.

He tried to corner Kiara but she snubbed him and rushed back to join her friends. A peeved Rahul, now began to eye her more vindictively.

At the stroke of midnight when Rishaan cut his birthday day cake with Kiara by his side, he had absolutely no idea about the drama that was to follow almost instantly. The moment Rishaan fed the first piece of cake to Kiara, one of the guests at the disc, not a part of Rishaan's party, took over the mike to make an announcement. To Kiara's shock, it was Rahul.

'Ladies and Gentleman, I would like to wish Kiara's new boyfriend, Rishaan, a very Happy Birthday. Rishaan, my boy, you are lucky to have Kiara in your life. As her ex, I can vouch that she is really good. All the best, dude!'

This rather obnoxious announcement by Rahul embarrassed the hosts to no end. It was evident that everybody around found it to be in rather cheap taste. And one look at Rahul, left the crowd with not the best impressions about Kiara.

Kiara ignored Rahul and turned to Rishaan.

'Happy Birthday, darling! I love you.'

Partly on an impulse and partly to hit back at Rahul, Kiara kissed Rishaan publically. And hence for nearly a minute, the guests gathered there witnessed a rather unexpected spurt of passion. Rahul walked away, looking rather flustered, while Rishaan stood annoyed at this rather impulsive public display of affection.

When Rishaan and Kiara withdrew themselves, they found it sheepish to have the entire disc gaze at them in disbelief. But among the crowd of guests, she had spotted someone very special, someone who had known her stupidities for far too long: Diya Kohli, her BFF, her buddy from school.

'Diya!' she screamed in joy and rushed to her.

Diya and Kiara hugged each other, even as Rishaan observed Diya from a distance, walking slowly towards the girls.

'Well, even though I am dead tired, I couldn't stop myself from dropping in for a bit and wishing my best friend's fiancé on his birthday,' Diya explained. 'Besides, I was dying to see you Kiara.' The girls hugged again.

'Meet my knight in shining armour, my reason to smile and the reason I don't crib about love anymore,' Kiara introduced Rishaan to Diya.

'Happy Birthday, Rishaan,' Diya wished him.

'Thank you. I have heard so much about you.'

'Oh, and in the last few months Kiara has only spoken about you.'

As they shook hands, Rishaan could not help but notice the sparkle on Diya's weary countenance. Despite the turmoil she seemed to be going through, a broad customary smile stood firm on her face. She carried immense positive vibes that made Rishaan forget some of the unpleasant moments of the evening. Kiara requested Rishaan to be with Diya, while she bade farewell to the guests and wound up the party. Although Rishaan was still very apprehensive about the idea of Diya staying with them, he did not seem to mind spending some time with this rather endearing stranger.

For the next half an hour, until the party wound up, Rishaan spent his time chatting with Diya and giving her company, while Kiara got back to entertaining the guests. Apart from the emotional turmoil that Diya was going through, she also seemed to be battling a particularly aggressive bout of migraine. Rishaan was at his caring best, putting her at ease and making sure she ate properly before popping a Saridon. He was also particularly careful with broaching a personal topic, and chose to avoid it altogether. Kiara was quite impressed looking at Rishaan attending to Diya's needs. 'Sure, Rishaan had multiple idiosyncrasies but he was also extremely compassionate,' she thought. After all, there was no reason for Rishaan to give Diya this kind of attention other than her being Kiara's best friend.

Rishaan hoped Kiara would wind up the party quickly, seeing Diya's jaded condition. But Kiara, true to her spirited self, continued to celebrate, oblivious of the severity of Diya's migraine. Rishaan reminded Kiara to wrap up the party as soon as possible. To which Kiara agreed, but in no time got drawn into a conversation with someone and forgot about it altogether. By the time the party got over, it was already 1.30 a.m. Rishaan wondered how Kiara could be this callous and irresponsible.

As Rishaan drove the car, a partially sloshed Kiara by his side and an unwell Diya on the backseat, his thoughts went back to the night's party and how it was more of a 'Kiara's-night-out-with-friends'. When suddenly his eyes shifted to the rear-view mirror wherein he could see Diya. Her eyes shut, Diya rested on the back seat. The dim light from the streets occasionally fell on the loose strand of hair, gently stroking her left cheek. Even with the pain searing inside, she looked an amazing picture of equanimity and calm. Throughout the drive, Rishaan kept looking at her, enamoured by her endearing persona. He wondered what kept his eyes glued to the rear view mirror. It was only a couple of days ago that Rishaan was dead against Diya staying with them.

As soon as they reached home, an exhausted Diya went straight to the spare bedroom and crashed in there. A good sleep was perhaps her best chance of escaping the migraine fury.

Rishaan was a sleepy. But Kiara, who was all charged up after the party, seemed to have other plans in mind. She was feeling horny, and as usual was all set to have her way. When she initiated, or rather, ignited physical indulgence with her deft, deadly moves which she knew Rishaan was ill-equipped to resist, the result had to be no different. Within minutes, Rishaan was ready to enter her. Rishaan, who started off rather reluctantly, ended on a high note. After the act was over, Kiara dozed off, while he remained awake battling his own dilemmas. Did Kiara allow him no say? Was he just playing along for reasons that weren't clear in his head?

For a long time, Rishaan kept mulling over such thoughts with clarity eluding him. Frustrated, he then got up to go to the washroom. As he crossed Diya's room, he was taken aback by a particularly unnerving sound coming from inside. Diya seemed to be in some sort of pain. She was breathing heavily and also giving out those gasps of discomfort that accompany breathlessness. Rishaan rushed inside to find her in a particularly bad state. She desperately needed her nebulizer, which she was unable to take out from her suitcase. Rishaan helped her with the needful just in the brink of time before her helplessness got the better of her.

'Migraine and asthma?' Rishaan asked in sheer surprise, when things seemed to have settled down.

'Yes, I've got both. They have made my life miserable since I was a kid. In fact, in the last couple of months there has been an addition to the list,' she smiled, somewhat apologetically.

'What's that?'

'Thanks to the mental turbulence I have been going through, I have been experiencing insomnia. On one occasion, I even sleepwalked. I just hope it does not happen again. It scares the shit out of me.'

'Hmm... That's quite a long list, indeed!'

With the asthma attack sorted, Rishaan decided to fix Diya's migraine problem. He had heard that an ice pack gives much relief during migraine attacks. He took the ice pack from the fridge and applied it on her forehead for a good 15 minutes. Much to his surprise, the trick actually worked. And a little while later, Diya too fell asleep.

It was already 4 in the morning and Rishaan felt too weary to move. Besides, having seen Diya in that vulnerable state, he was really scared: What if the attack recurred without him or Kiara knowing? As a hypochondriac himself, he had all sorts of delusions attack him fairly often. Hence, he rested himself on the sliding chair in Diya's room and tried sleeping there itself.

As he battled to sleep in vain, his eyes caught an old red-colour album hanging out of Diya's suitcase. In the frenzy to get her nebulizer out, she had scattered her things around. An inquisitive Rishaan took the album out and had a good look at it. The album was a rather exhaustive one: it had nearly two hundred pictures which perhaps contained Diya's life story. It had pictures of her as a toddler with a couple, who seemed like her parents, by her side. In one particular picture, she was laughing her heart out as her Dad, swung her in the air. But as Diya grew slightly older the couple disappeared from the pictures and so did that carefree laughter. Instead, in came another couple with two young girls. From the later pictures it seemed that Diya had been sent to a boarding school when she was pretty young. Henceforth, Kiara seemed to be there in most of her pictures. These pictures, that had Kiara and Diya together, were taken at different places: from the basketball court and swimming pool to their hostel rooms and excursion trips. In one picture, Diya was captured participating in a beauty contest. Rishaan remembered that Kiara had mentioned once that Diya had explored modelling as an option and even made it to the finals of the Miss India contest a few years ago. There was a picture in which Kiara was dressed in a traditional Benarasi saree and had adorned really expensive jewellery. In the backdrop, Rishaan could see a half-visible board that read DIYA WEDS... There were some outstanding pictures of the snow-clad Canadian countryside. But there was no picture of the guy Diya married. The omission seemed deliberate. Diya perhaps wanted to eliminate some years of her life: more likely, the ones when she was married.

The more Rishaan gazed through these pictures, the more he got entangled in her persona. He seemed to be vicariously living her journey as reflected in the photographs. There was something very endearing about her. Perhaps it was her stoic smile of reconciliation, which she wore uniformly in all the pictures and which circumvented the pressures of the circumstances in which they were clicked. There was something very attractive about her femininity. She seemed to be a strong, calm woman, who was firmly in control of her life despite the chaos. Rishaan was tempted to compare her with women who invited chaos in otherwise peaceful lives. It wasn't too difficult to figure out who he was possibly comparing Diya with, even if subconsciously so. Lost, Rishaan finally dozed off.

Fourteen

The heart wants what it wants. There's no logic to these things.
You meet someone and you fall in love and that's that.
—WOODY ALLEN

Diya brought in lots of positive vibes to Rishaan and Kiara's home. There was something very affirmative about her, especially her ability not to be cowed down by adversities.

Diya was used to waking up early in the morning at around 5. Then for nearly an hour and half she meditated and practised yoga. She pursued it diligently six days a week. One day when Rishaan woke up around 5.30 to go to the washroom, he caught a glimpse of Diya in a difficult yogic posture and was simply mesmerized by the effortlessness. Rishaan surmised that the inherent serenity he saw in her could perhaps be attributed to this 'spiritual discipline'. As a groggy Rishaan watched Diya from outside the door, she too, while changing her posture, caught him looking at her. Rishaan instantly gestured a thumbs up to her and moved on to his room.

From the next day Rishaan found himself waking up by 5. He would be restless for a while and kept turning sides before falling asleep again. But finally he gave into his anxiety when on the third day he again found himself awake that early. He decided not to suppress his natural instincts. He went to the other room where Diya was practicing yoga, and waited for a few minutes for her to open her eyes. But when she did not move, he broke her spell.

'I want to learn yoga. Will you teach me?'

For the next half an hour, Diya helped Rishaan perform some breathing exercises before they got down to doing the surya namaskar. And while they were performing surya namaskars together, Kiara walked into the room. She was surprised to see them perform yoga together. And after much ado, she reluctantly gave in. A sly smile escaped Rishaan on seeing the extra effort Kiara had to put in, in order to match steps with him and Diya. Kiara had missed the extra glow on Rishaan's face, a glow that had to be attributed to the positive energy the stranger had pumped in him.

Later in the day when Kiara was off to work and Rishaan was working on yet another draft of his script, he found himself repeatedly distracted by his thoughts about Diya. Why was he evincing so much interest in her? Why did everything about her seem so fascinating? Was he in awe of her? Was he finding himself drawn to her? Rishaan's rumination ended on an abrupt note when he got a call from a friend who was working as the chief assistant director with the critically acclaimed, Ranjan Bhatt.

'Hey Rishaan, congrats man! I heard you're doing a movie with Akash Jha.'

'Thanks, buddy. Yes, I am.'

'Listen, do you have a woman centric script. Something

that espouses a social cause and can be made within a budget of 4–5 crores? We have the dates of Bishakha De but don't quite have the right script for her?'

'No buddy. I'm afraid I don't have any such script.'

Bishaka was an ageing sex symbol who had been hunting for meaningful roles to sustain her career.

Rishaan was pleasantly surprised that, like him, even Diya would spend her entire day locked up in her room either reading or writing something. She avoided talking about it. One afternoon when Rishaan found himself in a particularly distracted mood, he decided to unravel the mystery behind her secretive writings.

'What do you write Diya? Can I read it?' he asked from behind, almost surprising her.

'Not right now. I am not sure how much I want to tell and how much I want to conceal. Anyways, it is a depressing story.'

Although, she did inform him that she was writing a novel.

'It is inspired by what I have gone through in the last couple of years. Love, dominance, deception, betrayal...my story has it all,' she smiled bravely. 'I am halfway done. If I spend the next four weeks on it, it should be finished.'

'Hmm... Interesting. A gorgeous, intelligent woman who had it all, squandered it away, and is now writing about it.'

'I didn't squander it away. I believed in love. I believed in God.'

◆

That night when Rishaan hit the bed, Diya's words, 'I believed in love. I believed in God', kept echoing in his ears. She surely had a story to tell. And for some strange reason, he seemed to feel he was a part of that story.

Much to Rishaan's surprise, he had begun to like his house much more in the last few days. And the reason was that things suddenly seemed a lot more organized. Until now, the cook would almost invariably end up cooking parathas for breakfast, simply because both Rishaan and Kiara were too lazy to shop for stuff for breakfast. Now, Diya took it upon herself to set a breakfast menu, and made sure that things needed for breakfast were in place. And when the cook bunked, she would take charge of the kitchen and treat Rishaan and Kiara to delicious food.

'I find cooking therapeutic,' she would tell Rishaan and Kiara. 'And trust me, I am not putting any effort into it. It just makes me feel good to think that the stuff I cooked, managed to bring a smile on someone's face.'

Much to his dislike, Rishaan again found himself drawing a comparison. He wondered if drinking was all Kiara found therapeutic. The very next moment though, he snubbed himself for the nasty thought.

One afternoon, Rishaan, who had just begun working on a new script, found himself stuck on the very first scene where the hero and heroine get introduced to each other. He battled with his thoughts for a good two hours till he decided it just wasn't meeting his satisfaction. Sitting on his chair, as he stretched his arms and legs, partly to ensure a good circulation of blood and partly to beat the monotony, he was surprised to see Diya walk in with a cup of green tea for him.

'Have it. You seem so stressed that I could hear your irritated gasps even from the other room,' she said, holding out the tea cup for him.

'Would you mind hearing out a couple of scenes I have written?'

'Surely, but first tell me the story.'

'Well, the story is as simple as it is complicated.'

'Hmm...'

'It's a love story between a girl, who is a software engineer in one of India's topmost IT companies, and her boss, who heads a team of forty people.'

'And?'

'There's a catch. The boss is actually a RAW agent while the girl heads the IT cell of India's most dreaded terror group.'

'Wow! That's damn fascinating.'

In the next half an hour, Rishaan narrated to her his scenes and also discussed with her the plot. Much to his surprise, Diya gave him some great character inputs.

'Wow! I never knew you were so passionate about movies,' he remarked.

'Well, when I was studying psychology, I made it a point to watch a lot of thrillers and even murder mysteries. They served as an exercise for me. I used to guess the next moves of the main characters and analyse if the writer and director really understood the human mind.'

'Aha...so what's your opinion about me. Do I understand human psychology well?'

'Ummm... I guess you do.'

Rishaan found the interaction quite absorbing; it whetted up his interest to prolong the same in a more creatively conducive ambience, with the cloudy weather outside only serving as an inducement. Rishaan asked her if they could carry forth the discussion in a coffee shop.

Half an hour later, they sat at the Versova Barista. The gusty wind, that is so typical of a Mumbai monsoon, was so strong that afternoon, it seemed that the wind would blow them. Rishaan did not seem to mind the prospect.

It was only natural that in an ambience as distracting as this, the script narration would easily take a back seat.

'So how's your book coming along?' Rishaan asked her.

'It's okay. The writing has been a bit slow since the last three to four days.'

'Is it cumbersome to write about your depressing moments?'

'It is. But it is also an escape. By writing away your pain and hurt, you often exorcize them.'

'Does it hurt that bad?'

Rishaan realized the folly of his query the moment he had uttered those words. Diya didn't have an answer to that. She was on the verge of breaking down, with drops of tears flowing down her cheeks.

'I...I am sorry,' said Rishaan, rather apologetically. 'In a situation like this, you want to show you care and you often don't realize that the other person finds your care intrusive. I am sorry.'

Diya was quite taken in by his honesty. Rishaan offered her his handkerchief. After wiping her tears Rishaan and Diya got down to having the cappuccino. The conversation shifted to Kiara.

'It's amazing how Kiara and I are poles apart. There's nothing we have in common except perhaps that both of us are good souls,' Diya mentioned in passing.

It wasn't surprising that Rishaan was tempted to repeat

exactly the same words to describe his equation with Kiara. But he somehow refrained from doing so. Sipping his coffee, he wondered aloud rather pensively, 'Does just being good souls suffice in sustaining a relationship?'

The unsuspecting query had Diya think about it.

'Why do you ask that?' she counter-questioned him, sounding a bit circumspect.

'Generally,' he said, somewhat diffidently.

A sudden gush of rain brought a welcome relief to a somewhat tricky conversation. As it rained outside, Diya and Rishaan abandoned the talk and instead just soaked in the lovely, refreshing ambience. Right at that point, Rishaan got an unexpected call. It was from Subhankar, the HR consultant whom Kiara had befriended in the gym.

'Dude, I've got an excellent opportunity for you!' said Subhankar.

'Opportunity?'

'Yes. Sony TV is looking for a creative director. And I think your profile ideally fits the bill. The remuneration is almost double of what you were getting at Star.'

The offer irritated Rishaan, for by now it was pretty clear in his head that he was not interested in another job.

'Subhankar, I am not interested at this stage. My independent career as scriptwriter is taking off, and I'd much rather concentrate on that.'

'In that case, there is another opportunity with a production house. It is of a media consultant. The job would offer you flexible timings and roughly the same perks you enjoyed at Star.'

It is strange how a creative guy like Rishaan is often

compelled to choose between money and passion. Of late, when somebody offered Rishaan a job, it actually offended him more than making him feel good. He felt that his capabilities of making it on his own were being doubted. So when Subhankar tried to be a bit persuasive, Rishaan blew a fuse.

'Listen Subhankar, did I tell you that I need a job? Then you have no business calling me and telling me what I should be doing with my career,' he chided Subhankar rather assertively.

'You didn't, dude. But your resume was mailed to me by Kiara.'

Rishaan was shocked when he heard this and immediately disconnected the phone. He had had enough for the day.

Later that night, Rishaan and Kiara had a major skirmish.

'Kiara, in future you don't need to mail my resume to anyone. In fact, just delete it from your laptop,' he snubbed her.

Kiara, who had had an argument with her boss that evening and was in a foul mood too, shot back rather uncharacteristically.

'Stop throwing this attitude, Rishaan. Whatever I did was for your good. In the last five months, all you've earned is this cheque of ₹1.5 lakhs. Just think about it. Consulting with a production house is definitely not a bad idea.'

'Kiara, you knew I wanted a year to focus on my scriptwriting career. And you also know that I have managed a big break, something not many manage this early. Then what's your problem? What's bugging you?'

Kiara looked a bit uncertain before she replied, 'Rishaan if we have to get married in a year's time, we need a better bank balance. We need more inflow of money to invest in a house of our own. Besides, you know how uncertain the film industry is. What if your financier does an about-turn and refuses to put money on Asif Khan? In that case, your movie will be stuck once again.'

Rishaan lost his cool completely when he heard this.

'Damnit! Who has set this deadline of marriage within a year's time? Listen, if you love me, you have got to support me in my dreams. If you can't, the choice is entirely yours.' Saying thus, he stormed out of the room.

'Of course! And I have no right to expect you to support mine,' Kiara yelled back, even as he was leaving.

'Oh! Come on! You don't have any dreams except for making more money. You don't have any creative aspirations. Nor do you have the capacity to understand those who have it in them,' he retorted from outside the room.

Kiara banged the door shut. After a bad day in office, she had no energy to fight with Rishaan. It hurt her to think that Rishaan should misunderstand her, when everything she did was keeping his and their future in mind.

At 12.30 in the night, Rishaan sat alone gazing outside the window and counting the lights he could see at the far end of the sea. In depressing moments like these, he tended to count the number of boats that were still out for fishing in the sea. This helped him temporarily forget the chaos inside him. But this argument had been so unnerving that the trick simply didn't seem to work.

Why was Kiara behaving in such a selfish way? When he first met her, she didn't even seem the types who would be serious about marriage. Then how come this sudden change? Did she love him so much? Then why couldn't she see things from his point of view? And if she didn't love him, was it purely her insecurities and the fear of another heartbreak that was making her cling on to him?

As Rishaan gazed out of the window, he suddenly heard some commotion behind him. Much to his surprise, he found Diya up and about. He saw her open the main door.

'Diya, where are you going?' he called after her.

Diya went on, ignoring him. It was then that it struck Rishaan that she was perhaps sleepwalking. Rishaan followed close behind her inquisitively.

Diya took the lift. Rishaan entered behind her. He stood right beside her, without her even realizing it. She walked out of the society premises, Rishaan closely following her, meaning to understand her ailment a little better. Diya walked out of the main gate and had begun to cross the road when Rishaan finally got alarmed. Even at 1 in the night, there was enough traffic on the streets for something tragic to happen. He rushed behind her only to see her headed for a collision with a speeding SUV. He ran and pulled her back just in the nick of time before being run over. The jerk finally got Diya out of her sleep.

'Diya, what were you doing? Do you realize you would have been knocked down?'

'I...I...I just felt like sitting in the coffee shop for a while,' she said innocently, fumbling for words.

It took her a few moments to realize that Rishaan had saved her life. And when she realized it, she felt really sorry and thankful at the same time. Rishaan held her hand and brought her home with a lot of care and affection. He sat by her side for some time, trying to put her to sleep.

'Relax, Rishaan. You need to go and sleep. I am fine. I

will manage,' she said, convincing him to leave.

Even as Diya pondered over what had just happened, she couldn't help wondering if destiny had planned to make them spend more time with each other. Rishaan seemed so different from her devil-like husband, Derek. In a passing thought, she feared that if she spent more time with Rishaan, she might start trusting men again.

Diya knew that for her to be happy, she had to keep the mistrust alive.

Fifteen

The greatest relationships are the ones
you never expected to be in.

The next morning, Diya was off to meet her bua in Chembur. She started off from home quite early, leaving Kiara and Rishaan alone at the breakfast table. It was an awkward breakfast meeting for the couple, especially as the skirmish of the previous night wasn't out of their minds. While Kiara was thinking about their flight, Rishaan was distracted by the images of Diya sleepwalking the previous night.

'Rishaan, I am sorry about last night,' Kiara broke the silence.

Her words brought Rishaan out of his reverie. But he remained quiet, making Kiara add an explanation.

'I understand that I was being unfair to you. You need time to pursue your dreams. You know what, my parents' divorce has left an indelible scar on me. It has made me so insecure. I fear that I might lose you. I fear I might lose this little world of happiness that I have managed to create with you in the last few months. And yes that sometimes makes me act a bit selfish, as you say.'

Rishaan heard her patiently before responding.

'Have I given you reasons to feel insecure?'

For a moment, Kiara did not know how to react to this unusually blunt query. She shook her head.

'And yes, I wanted to tell you that Diya will move out soon so that you don't face any more disturbances. In fact, I have put her in touch with a couple of property agents.'

The information took Rishaan by surprise.

'Ah...well...what's the hurry? Let her stay here for some time if she feels comfortable.'

'Are you sure?'

'Y...y...yeah.'

After Kiara left for office, for the first time since the two moved in together, Rishaan was feeling lonely in his own house.

As he gazed into the firmament, a myriad thoughts flooded his mind: him seeing her for the first time at the party, then observing her on the rear view mirror, helping her fight the twin attacks—migraine and asthma, putting her to sleep, flipping through her album, watching her practise yoga, narrating his script to her, having coffee with her amidst heavy rains, salvaging her from her sleepwalking state and pulling her away from a near fatal situation. Why were her thoughts suddenly so addictive? Why did the stranger suddenly seemed so dangerously familiar?

With little control over his wandering mind, Rishaan went into Diya's room and did what he would never dare to have done. He knew where Diya kept the printouts of the manuscript she had been working on. He took it out and started reading it.

Diya was born to a Punjabi father and a Tamil mother, who had fallen in love with each other in college. Her father was a pilot and her mother a classical singer. They lived in Green Park Extension, a posh locality in South Delhi. Diya's parents had a crazy knack for adventure, which is probably why the two fell for each other in the first place. When Diya was two-and-a-half years old, they went on a month long trek to the Kailash Mansarovar, leaving the toddler Diya with her grandmother. Unfortunately, they never returned from the trip. An avalanche had consumed the entire group of 50 odd people. Diya's grandmother got to know of the mishap only a week after it had occurred. But Little Diya had sensed the fate of her parents even before the world got to know about it. For the three days, around the time the mishap is believed to have taken place, Diya hardly ate, cried rather fearfully and had these abrupt bouts of sweating which neither her grandmother nor her doctor could fathom.

An year later, Diya's grandmother also passed away. She could never get over the trauma of losing her son and daughter-in-law. Subsequently, Diya was adopted by her bua, her father's sister, who lived with her husband, a businessman by profession, and two daughters in Pritampura, West Delhi. Diya's uncle owned a fleet of tourist buses. As such, money was never a problem in the family. The problem was in their lack of finesse. Her bua was essentially a very jealous soul, who would find it tough to say anything good about anybody. Even when she spoke about Diya's deceased mother, she spoke in a somewhat taunting, sarcastic manner. Diya simply hated her bua for this. The bua would often draw comparisons between

Diya and her daughters. Diya was any day more beautiful and better at studies than her bua's daughters. Her cousins were often snubbed by their parents for not being 'as good'. As a result of this mindless competition, the cousins grew up hating Diya. When the bua was not around, they would bully her, even deprive her of food. They made Diya do their homework and run around for their errands. And when she failed to live up to their whims, they abused and scared her. In a conflict between the kids, bua no doubt always took her kids' side; and the bua's husband was too busy to bother.

When Diya was ten years old, her maasi, who lived in London, visited her. The maasi spent a whole day with Diya in the hotel where she was putting up. She was shocked to find that the jovial, happy-go-lucky Diya had become an extremely withdrawn, unhappy kid, who seldom smiled or spoke freely. It did not take her long to surmise the reasons behind it. She made an offer to the bua's family: to sponsor Diya's education in a boarding school. The bua thought it to be good riddance from Diya. At the same time, the bua did not want to lose all her control over Diya. 'Diya does have something special in her; who knows tomorrow she could get married in a very rich family,' the Bua would say manipulatively. Hence, the bua agreed to the maasi's proposal only on the condition that she and her husband be listed as Diya's guardians.

And so, eleven-years-old Diya Kohli was sent to the Welham Girls' School in Dehradun to pursue her education. When she stepped into Welham, for the first time in many years she felt independent, something she had been deprived of for far too long at her bua's place. Gradually, Diya started opening up to people, she had made a couple of new friends, developed a flair for painting and showcased her prowess in basketball. Unlike most other students, she took the physical exercises far more seriously. At times, when she felt too lonely or low, she would go out for a run. The energy release helped her overcome many of those pressing worries.

A year later, Diya's life took a new turn when Kiara entered the boarding school. Kiara and Diya hit it off like some long lost bosom buddies. Even at 12, the two girls were distinctively more gorgeous and way more attractive than others in the school. One was the traditional, blue-eyed fairy while the other was a dusky damsel in the making. But what really helped them bond so well was perhaps the feeling of 'incomplete parenting'. The absence of Diya's parents had left a void in her life that could never be filled; on the other hand, after going through her parents' acrimonious divorce, Kiara for long had to cope with a sense of deep-rooted anger.

Together, the two learnt to blow away their stress in sweet nothings. They bunked classes to watch movies: Diya for Shah Rukh and Kiara for Salman. They enjoyed playing basketball so much that within months they were knocking the doors of the school team. They were room-mates in hostel. While Diya was more disciplined of the two, washing her clothes daily and carrying out personal chores on time, Kiara was incorrigibly lazy.

Like all best friends Kiara and Diya often swapped their dresses. And hence in their limited budget, they managed a great variety of dresses. Kiara, on one occasion, even usurped Diya's hot red underwear which she really liked.

From books to sports, from food to dresses, from joys to sorrows, Kiara and Diya were soul mates meant to help each other accumulate those well-deserved happiness which they had been unfairly deprived of.

As a relationship grows, it also goes through many ebbs and flows. It was time for their relationship to face the test of fire.

Two years later, the first misunderstanding between Diya and Kiara arose during the annual school 'Socials'. A party specific to class IX and X students was organized every year between the girls of Welham and the boys of a neighbouring all-boys school. This was an event that every heterosexual student of the two schools would eagerly look forward to the day he or she entered class IX.

In the party, Diya found herself particularly attracted to a lanky, long-haired guy called Pranav. Twice she tried broaching a conversation with him, but to her surprise found him rather unresponsive. An hour later while she mingled with another group, she was surprised to see Pranav and Kiara chatting all alone in a corner..

That night, Kiara and Diya had a bit of a tiff over this guy.

'Come on Kiara, you knew I had a soft corner for Pranav,' Diya protested.

'Yeah, but he didn't,' she said, sounding rather indifferent.

'What do you mean? Is that how sensitive you are towards my feelings?'

'Oh come on, Diya. Don't make a mountain out of molehill. I didn't go to him like you did. He came to me and started showering praises. I am not stupid to tell him to get lost.'

Kiara and Pranav dated for almost a month. They would meet in the evenings after their classes got over and hung out for a couple of hours before returning to their hostels. On some occasions, they indulged in some kissing and necking too.

For the entire month, Kiara and Diya were not on the best of terms. Diya had tried mending things with Kiara, but had failed to do so.

One evening, Kiara walked in carrying a box of chocolates for Diya.

'What's all this for?' Diya asked, rather indifferently.

'Pranav and I broke up,' she announced happily. 'The bastard already has a girlfriend in Delhi. He just wanted some extra fun on the sly.'

'What? Aren't you upset?' Diya asked, a bit shocked at Kiara's casual reconciliation.

'Ah! Well, I always knew it was a temporary thing with him. You really think one should involve herself seriously at this age?'

Kiara, had always been the practical sorts. At 15, she knew exactly the degree of indulgence and the measure of involvement she could give to a relationship. Diya, on the other hand, was always the emotional sorts, who clung on to people she was fond of for as long as possible. She believed in her instincts and seldom manoeuvred them to suit the ways of the world.

A few days later, Kiara and Diya were back to being the best of friends. Diya had put behind the betrayal simply because Kiara meant a lot to her. She did not want to hold grudges against someone who had brought so much happiness into her life.

A couple of weeks later, Kiara and Diya were off on a school excursion to Goa. There Kiara and a couple of girls had their first brush with 'grass' on a secluded beach in North

Goa. Diya was also present, but firmly resisted the lure.

On the last day of their Goa trip, Kiara came up with yet another spunky, crazy idea. She got two gorgeous pair of bikinis—one for her and the other for Diya. She wanted Diya and herself to be clicked together on the beach giving the best of modelling poses. As they hunted for someone who would do the job, they came across this Spanish hunk of about 6ft 2 inches in his yellow swimming trunks. The Spaniard was very amiable and most willing to oblige. For the next half an hour, Kiara and Diya were clicked giving the best of poses, each vying for the handsome Spanish's attention.

When they were finally done, Kiara and Diya were spellbound looking at the amazing pictures he had clicked. They asked him out for dinner, only to discover that he was gay and was already booked for a dinner date with someone.

Goa had always been their best trip and those pictures were their 'best kept secret'.

Soon it was time for Kiara and Diya to go to college. They remained the best of friends even there. Both did their graduation from the Lady Shri Ram College, Kiara in commerce and Diya in English Literature. During college, Diya was encouraged and persuaded by a friend's brother, who was a fashion photographer, to have her portfolio clicked.

'You've got the right fusion of looks. The best of the East and the West. If you're lucky, you could go as far as Aishwarya Rai,' he'd tell her.

The fact that Diya could never feel a sense of belongingness with her her bua or maasi made her wanting to earn as quickly as possible. Hence, without informing her bua's family, she got her portfolio clicked. The driving force behind it was to earn a quick buck and attain some kind of financial independence. As luck would have it, her portfolio took her to the finals of Miss India Contest. Despite some cribbing and emotional blackmail from her bua's side, she knew that in her heart of hearts, the calculative bua would want her to compete and win the contest. After all, if she won, the financial stakes for the bua would be very high.

Though Diya could not finish in the top 5, the very fact that she could be in top 25 boosted her confidence manifolds. She did get a couple of modelling assignments subsequently: a print ad for a pen and a TVC for a clothing brand. But given the uncertainty she had lived with ever since she lost her parents, she wanted more stability in her life. Her bua's family was anyways very unhappy with her modelling aspirations.

'Either you make it really big and mint lots of money or you quit. No point hanging midway,' her bua would often tell her, faking concern.

Diya's own sensibilities also restricted her options. And six months after graduation, while she was still getting offers to walk the ramp, she took up a six months training with an institute that groomed air hostesses. And soon after, she was flying with the British Airways.

Soon after completing her graduation, Kiara too got herself enrolled in an MBA college in Pune. This marked the end of a long and happy journey where Kiara and Diya finally went their separate ways. They kept in touch via mails and through a social networking site called Orkut, pretty popular in those days.

Diya quite enjoyed the financial independence the job gave her. Unlike Kiara, she wasn't someone who would draw up long term plans for herself. She was happy in escaping from her personal hassles by smiling at strangers on the flight. Flying thousands of feet above the earth helped her forget many of the issues she'd otherwise have to face when on land.

A few months later, on a flight from London to New York, Diya caught the fancy of a handsome thirty-year-old, Indo-Canadian businessman, Derek Singh, who was settled in Hamilton, Canada. Nearly forty years ago, Derek's father had migrated to Canada from Ludhiana where he set up an electronic shop and married a Canadian girl. By the time Derek grew up, they had ventured into the cable TV business and even become one of the leading cable TV distributors in Canada. Hence, Derek lived an opulent life with very little inspiration to try and achieve something on his own.

For Derek, it was love at first sight when he saw Diya or so he made her believe. The first time she served him food on the aircraft, he simply could not take his eyes off her.

'Would you like a fruit juice or a soft drink?' she asked him.

'Will you feed me like this every day?' he asked her.

'Sorry?'

'I want you to be in front of my eyes all the time.'

Diya thought he was a psychopath and requested another hostess to attend to him. He kept looking at her, unfazed for the next few hours till the flight finally landed. While leaving the aircraft, as Diya stood at the exit, he told her, 'We shall meet again very soon.'

A day later when Diya was flying back to London, she was shocked to find Derek in the same flight.

'Ah well, I managed to find out that you'd be flying in

this flight.' He smiled.

Diya ignored him and walked on. For the next two hours, he kept gazing at her in a lovelorn manner. Unable to take this ogling anymore, Diya asked him to come to a quiet place just outside the washroom.

'What do you want from me?' she asked him in a hushed tone.

He took out a ring from his pocket, bent on his knees and gestured for her ring finger. Diya was just shell-shocked, unable to figure out how she should react. Right at that point, an eighty-year-old woman, who had stepped out of the toilet, looked mesmerized to see what was happening in front of her.

'Come on child, give him your hand. I have seen the whole world and I can see it in his eyes how much he loves you,' she prodded Diya.

And before Diya could react, Derek took her hand somewhat firmly and put the ring on it. Much to her surprise, she did not protest at the moment. Was she subconsciously liking the sense of ownership this dude exercised on her? After all, one of the deepest regrets in her life had been of not belonging to anybody?

Before alighting from the flight, Diya went to Derek and asked him to keep the ring.

'Throw it in the dustbin if you like, but don't ask me to take my love back,' he told her, rather obsessively. 'At least meet me for an hour at a coffee shop before shutting me out,' he pleaded with her.

That evening after landing in London, Derek and Diya met at a coffee shop. Derek told her about his family and Diya about the absence of her's.

What surprised Diya was that Derek had never been in a relationship before.

'I had always been looking for that Indian girl who would sweep me off my feet at the very first sight. Finally I have found one.'

Diya remained sceptical and unsure. There were two things she had to take a call on. Was she prepared for marriage? Was she prepared for marriage with Derek? The first dilemma was of course more critical, considering that as someone who did not expect much from the world nor really belonged to those who had brought her up, she'd be happy to go ahead with someone who really loved her.

For a month Diya tried to gauge Derek's intentions. She interacted with him but only when he called her; Derek would call her at least twice daily. He said he wanted to share his life with her. And also wanted her to open up to him. Three weeks later, he landed in London just to spend more time with her. They went out for a weekend dinner and later watched a movie together. On this visit Diya found Derek more familiar and less of a stranger.

Two weeks later Diya came to India for a small holiday. By now her bua's family had shifted to Mumbai. Very hesitantly she confided about Derek to her bua. She had feared that the bua would snub her.

'Are they really rich? And is he good looking?' she queried..

For a moment, the bua, who was struggling to find the right match for her elder daughter, was tempted to pitch her own daughter to Derek. But when she heard just how far he had gone for Diya, she aborted the thought.

'Can we meet Derek?' she asked Diya.

Three days later, Derek flew in from Canada to meet Diya's family. The urgency in his demeanour surprised Diya's folks and convinced him that he actually loved her.

'In any case, a Canadian connection is always good. Derek's ancestors come from the same village in Ludhiana as mine. Who knows, his father might help us set up a base in Canada. And in any case, you won't have to worry about arranging Diya's marriage,' the bua's husband told her after meeting Derek.

It was only after her bua's nod for the marriage that it dawned upon Diya just how close she was to a life altering moment. In her nervousness, she travelled to Pune to have a chat with Kiara.

'Ultimately, it all boils down to what you really want, Diya,' Kiara advised her.

'And that is what I don't seem to know,' Diya replied. In an after thought, she added, 'But I guess I always wanted to settle far away from the people I grew up with. I wanted to start a new life in a new world.'

'In that case, this is your opportunity.'

Two months later, Diya and Derek got married in the month of February on what seemed to be one of the most humid February days that Mumbai had witnessed in a long time. Perhaps the weather was preparing her for the greater extremes she'd have to negotiate with in Canada; two days later, from the 37 degrees temperature in Mumbai, Diya was battling a -26 in Canada. Her life too witnessed an equally humongous change.

Derek was indeed too sweet to be true. And when his real, diabolic self came to the fore, Diya knew her future was doomed.

♦

Rishaan flipped to the next page and found the pages washed out and a couple of them torn into two or three parts. Was it Diya's tears which she couldn't hold back? Was it so depressing from here on that she could not bear to read her own story and hence tore it off?

Rishaan decided not to make the extra effort of deciphering the torn pages. He'd much rather hear it from Diya. Whatever he had read about Diya's life, was enough to haunt him for some time. He could vividly visualize many of those moments lived by Diya. He wondered why he felt so empathetic towards her.

That night Diya stayed over at her bua's in Chembur. Kiara came home to inform Rishaan that she'd be off the next morning to Delhi on a three-day official assignment. But post that, she had a surprise planned for the weekend.

'My college friend, Swati from Goa, is getting married in Panjim on Sunday. I didn't quite intend to go but since most of my batchmates are going to be there, can we plan a short trip to Goa over the weekend?' Kiara asked Rishaan, somewhat sceptically, not sure about his reaction.

'Well, I have to work on a new script. Why don't you go? Maybe you could take Diya along?' he suggested, weighing different options at hand.

'Cool...I'll think about it.'

Kiara, who seemed a bit more relaxed, partly at the prospect of spending the weekend in Goa and partly due to the privacy regained by Diya's absence, got into the foreplay. Rishaan, on the other hand, was distracted and not in his elements.

As she smothered his neck and chest with her kisses, she asked him something that left him aghast. 'Are you thinking about Diya?'

For a moment, Rishaan was stumped. He felt as if she could see through his thoughts.

'You really know how to psyche people up,' Rishaan warded off the query with a smile.

'There's nothing wrong if she is playing on your mind. She indeed has a very resplendent personality.'

Saying thus, Kiara smooched Rishaan. Rishaan, who normally liked this sexual-dominance of his partner, was compelled to wonder if today the dominance carried an element of angst in it. Extricating her lips from the smooch, Kiara was ready with her next query.

'Where did the two of you go last night?'

'Oh, so you were following us,' Rishaan replied, kissing her shoulder and consciously avoiding a direct eye contact.

'Just being inquisitive,' she said, lighting a cigarette in front of him after many weeks, as though out of rebellion.

Rishaan told her everything that had happened: Diya's sleepwalking problem, her breathlessness coupled with severe migraine.

'Ah...well...she needs support. I am glad you followed her,' said Kiara.

Rishaan wasn't particularly in the mood to prolong the act. Stubbing the cigarette, he worked himself up to reach orgasm quickly. The moment consummation happened, Rishaan realized that he had never felt so detached while entering Kiara.

After the act was over, an exhausted Kiara fell asleep.

Rishaan, on the other hand, went back to his little work station in the living room. There he remained lost in the thoughts of the character and her turbulent journey. He could clearly visualize the way Diya's mean bua would make her childhood sad and unhappy. He could imagine Diya and Kiara fighting over Kiara's short-term boyfriend in school, the Goa trip, where the two vied for the attention of the handsome Spaniard and the crazy Indo-Canadain who fell in love with her. What intrigued him though were the events that followed, which were missing from the manuscript. Was it something so unnerving that even Diya couldn't read it?

He took his cellphone and started typing a message to his chief-assistant-director friend: *I think I have a script that fits your bill. Just give me a week and I should be ready for a narration.*

Rishaan took a deep breath and rested himself on his sliding chair. He started counting the small lights in the firmament. Deep within, he felt a searing pain waiting to be released.

Sixteen

You know it's love when all you want is that person to be happy, even if you're not part of their happiness.
—JULIA ROBERTS

Next morning when Kiara joined Rishaan at the breakfast table, she found him deeply engrossed in work. Kiara was ready to leave in some time with her suitcase by her side. She found it odd that Rishaan should be occupied with his stuff when she was leaving for three days.

'Rishaan, can we have breakfast together?' she asked, somewhat tersely.

Rishaan nodded disinterestedly, only making it tough for Kiara to contain her anger. He gave the print command while Kiara wondered what he was up to. He went to the printer, took the printouts and gave it to Kiara.

'Now what is this?' she asked, seeming somewhat irritated.

She looked at the paper. In her hand were printouts of their Goa plane tickets.

'Whoa! I love you,' she hugged him in excitement. 'I am so glad that you still manage to surprise me.'

'Anything for you, ma'am.' Rishaan smiled back.

Kiara looked at the tickets again. This time her ecstasy was replaced with a shade of concern.

'Are you sure Diya would be comfortable travelling with us?' she asked. 'I mean, did you check with her?'

'Ah...w...well, I thought, you'd like her to travel with us,' Rishaan replied nervously. 'If you don't want her to come with us, I can cancel her ticket.'

Kiara wasn't particularly happy. She wondered why the thought of having Diya at Goa irked her. After all, they had such fond memories from their last trip together.

'W...well...no, just let it be. It will be a nice break for Diya too,' Kiara said diffidently, though slightly confused at Rishaan's behaviour.

At that point, the doorbell rang. It was Diya; she was back from her aunt's place.

Kiara experienced an unusual feeling of forlornness as she left for the airport.

An hour later, as Rishaan sipped his green tea and Diya ate her breakfast, Rishaan said, 'Diya, would you mind coming with me to a coffee shop? I want to narrate a script to you.'

'Oh well, sure.'

Half an hour later when Rishaan and Diya left home, Rishaan drove to a distant Madh resort.

'Rishaan, we could have sat in any of the coffee shops nearby.' Diya said, a bit confused.

'Well, it's a script that requires very patient and peaceful hearing,' replied Rishaan, adding to her confusion.

Even after they occupied their seats at the sea-facing café, Rishaan was in no hurry to start the narration. He seemed a bit spaced out and unsure, prompting Diya to ask him to start.

With reasonable self-doubts, Rishaan narrated a story which seemed straight out of Diya's life. He dreaded to see how Diya would react after he completed his narration.

'Oh, so you read my manuscript?'

'I am earnestly sorry for that. But I have to confess that after reading it, I wanted to know about you beyond what you were ready to share.'

'Why so?'

'A writer is all about his characters. And for reasons I am not sure yet, your character fascinates me.'

'If you want to be a good writer, stop getting fascinated by tragic stories. My life has little in it beyond loss.'

'And that's precisely what draws my interest. Your story is about loss but you are not a loser.'

'You think so?'

'Yes.'

'Why?'

Rishaan could never get himself to tell her how much he was in awe of her stoicism, calmness and grace.

'Ah well, there is a certain vibrancy about you that doles out unending hope. It fills you up with optimism,' he reasoned, sounding more rational.

For the next few minutes, conversation remained sparse. Diya did not know what to make out of Rishaan's interest in her life. It boosted her self-esteem at times. But contrary to the stoic calmness she projected in front of the world, only she knew how fallible and fragile she could be. This time, she was also scared. Was she prepared to bare all—her thoughts, her feelings, her emotions, herself—in front of Rishaan?

'Diya I want to know that part of the story which you

probably tore off after writing. Your life in Canada. The one and half years you spent with Derek,' said Rishaan, with a sense of authority in his voice.

No, she wasn't prepared to talk about her life in Canada. She'd rather pen it down and let the world read it.

'Diya, just blurt it out. Trust me, you will feel unencumbered and a lot better,' Rishaan virtually exhorted her, looking straight into her eyes.

The turmoil on Diya's countenance was quite apparent now. She did not want to be rude but thought Rishaan to be too presumptuous for believing that she would feel comfortable sharing that part of her life, which she had shied away from sharing even with Kiara.

Rishaan kept looking into Diya's eyes, waiting for an answer when Diya suddenly turned towards the waiter passing by.

'Excuse me, can you get us the check please?' she said. 'Let's leave, Rishaan?'

The journey back home seemed a lot longer where the two remained absolutely quiet. While Diya mainly looked out of the window, Rishaan tried hard to concentrate on his driving. He couldn't help but wonder: had he been intrusive to the extent of jeopardizing the beautiful bond that had begun to develop between them?

That evening, Diya and Rishaan hardly spoke to each other. Diya was hooked to her writing and Rishaan was lost in his thoughts.

Left alone, Diya kept wondering why it was so difficult to write and get over with that part of her life. As she tried putting pen to paper, she forced herself to relive some of the extremely difficult moments, the ones she had been trying to exorcize.

Rishaan, for his part, sat in his room and looked at the tiny lights floating in the sea. He wondered if all was well with him. Why was he so insatiably curious about his girlfriend's best friend?

Next morning, when Rishaan entered the living room rubbing his sleepy eyes, he was surprised to find Diya sitting there properly dressed as though ready to head out somewhere.

'Rishaan, care to take me to the coffee shop we visited yesterday?' she said, surprising Rishaan completely.

Two hours later, Rishaan and Diya sat over piping hot café lattes. Diya was prepared to bare her heart and started right away.

'Soon after my marriage, I realized Derek was battling many complexes. His Canadian mother had ditched his father when he was only twelve years old. The incident left such a deep impact on him that from there on he could not trust any woman. He grew into a very insecure man. Due to his insecurities, he had never been in a relationship before. I was the first woman he had sex with.'

'And?'

'He couldn't have it.'

'What?'

'His constant insecurities had affected him psychologically. Halfway through the act, he would start behaving weird, almost as if he was suddenly angry with me. He would lose momentum and we'd end it abruptly.'

'Wasn't there a solution?'

'Well, the problem was in his mind. And hence, the cure

also had to be there. I tried a lot to talk to him, tried putting him at ease, but eventually I realized that he suffered from a condition which had him feel compulsively intimidated when in bed with a partner. The inherent anxieties frustrated him. Soon, situations arose wherein he'd suddenly get violent without any provocation. After which he would apologize continuously, coax me into sex, then fail again and soon unleash his anger on me.'

'Oh God! How long did this go on?'

'Almost six months.'

'And then?'

'He went to South America for four weeks on a business tour. When he returned, surprisingly he seemed a bit sorted and confident. For the first time, he managed to sustain the act and did it remarkably well. I was very happy. Things started looking up at last. For the next four months or so, we had great sex and even travelled on a holiday to Europe when things started falling apart again.'

At this point Diya choked with tears in her eyes. Rishaan patted her reassuringly and she continued with her story.

'One day, I discovered that Derek never went to South America. He had gone to Toronto to get himself treated by a sex therapist. As part of mental therapy session, the therapist had him sleep with whores. It gave Derek the confidence to perform the act. But given the jerk that he was, he developed a fascination for paid sex. After all, he was never short of money. When I confronted him, he abused me and told me not to mess with the happy situation we were in. I decided to reduce my expectations and keep a good distance from him. This further infuriated him.'

At that point, Rishaan got a call from Kiara. He was so absorbed in Diya's story that he ignored her calls twice and gestured to Diya to carry on.

'With time, the abuses increased. One night, he woke me from my sleep and wanted us to experiment with something crazy he had in his mind. I refused. The next morning, on the breakfast table, he splashed a cup of hot tea on my face. Another night when I was fast asleep, he got a flaming hot pan and slapped it on my back. I shrieked with pain. My back still carries the mark. I agree that I hoped for long that he mend his ways, but I had also begun contemplating about separation. The worst happened when one day he persuaded me to go for a weekend trip with his best friend, Mathew and his newly married wife, Katy. Later in the resort, I was stunned when he took me aside and told me, "We'll swap partners tonight. Mathew has the hots for you and will satisfy you like never before." I slapped him hard, not once but many times. He bled from the mouth. That day, I had lost all hopes of mending this relationship. This happened two weeks before I packed my bags and came down to India. We have agreed to go in for a mutual divorce. I will probably need to make a couple of trips back to Canada.'

By the time Diya had completed her story, she found it hard to control her emotions. Tears flowed down her cheeks and soon she was crying aloud in a rather cathartic manner. Rishaan hugged her reassuringly. As he did so, he could feel her body shivering. He felt a strange gush of empathy for her and hatred for her husband. A beautiful soul like Diya did not deserve to go through such pain.

Just as Diya finished telling her story, her cell phone rang.

It was Kiara. She was not in the frame of mind to take the call. By that time Rishaan, who had put his phone on the silent mode, realized that he had already missed four calls from Kiara.

Diya quickly gathered herself and called her back.

'Where are you, Diya? And where is Rishaan? I have called him so many times,' Kiara complained partly worried and partly irritated.

'Ah...well... Rishaan and I are at the Madh Resort coffee shop. Rishaan wanted to narrate a script.'

On hearing this Kiara's voice changed instantly.

'I see. And why the hell was he not taking my call? Just give the phone to him.'

Rishaan cooked up an excuse that his phone was on the silent mode and in the throes of narration he did not realize that she had called so many times. Kiara, for once, did not take the excuse at face value.

'Fair enough. Call me from the landline once you reach home.'

The emphasis on the landline was to ascertain what time Rishaan and Diya reached home. After keeping down the phone, Kiara felt very unusual. Of late she had been feeling her authority over Rishaan deplete. She had been rubbishing these thoughts, reasoning it to be a figment of her imagination. Well now she understood that it was not her imagination but her intuition that had been cajoling her.

Rishaan took Diya out for a walk in the pool-side garden abutting the sea. They watched the sun set, standing next to each other.

'That sunset perhaps symbolizes the closure of one chapter

of your life. The new is about to begin,' said Rishaan, trying to make her feel better. Little did he realize the uncanny resemblance of his words to the real-life situation between him and Diya.

Much after the sun had set and the stars were up, they sat on a bench facing the sea.

'Rishaan, you know what, to be honest, I am feeling much better after telling my story to you. Of late, I have led such a lonely existence that I do not feel like sharing my thoughts with anybody. I am glad I could do it with you.'

'I am glad you did Diya. I feel at peace too after hearing it,' said Rishaan, making her feel awkward.

'Should we go home? Kiara is expecting you to call back.' she said.

As they drove back, Rishaan looked a bit jittery. He was meaning to say something to Diya, but wasn't sure how to broach the conversation.

'Diya, I wanted to tell you something,' he said. 'A friend of mine had approached me a few days back asking for a woman-centric script for a small budget film. Before I heard about your traumatic experience with Derek, I had been a bit presumptuous and thought of requesting you to allow me to pitch your story as a film script. But not anymore. I think it's too personal an experience for you and too disturbing for me as a friend.'

Diya did not respond immediately. As they drove ahead, she finally put forth her thoughts.

'Rishaan, I think you should pitch it as a film script. I want it to get out of my system anyway. In fact, I can help you with the scripting.'

Rishaan nodded, without uttering a word. He held her hand reassuringly. For the first time, Diya could sense that his attachment with her was more than that of someone simply interested in her story. Had he developed an interest in her? She hoped not, but she neither had the patience nor the strength to mull over such a possibility.

The fact was that after her hellish experience in Canada, Diya did not mind spending long hours with someone as warm and pleasant as Rishaan. Was she aware of its obvious repercussions? She wasn't sure.

◆

Rishaan and Diya were in for a surprise when they reached home. The house was locked from inside. They rang the doorbell. To their surprise, it was Kiara.

'Hey, welcome back guys! It seems you two had a wonderful script reading session,' she cheered and then turned towards Rishaan. 'By the way, Rishaan, what a chhupa rustam you are! Are you really mentoring my friend or have you developed a crush on her? Huh?'

Kiara's blatant accusation had put Rishaan and Diya in an awkward situation. Kiara tried to make up for it by insisting that she was merely pulling their leg.

'A bad joke it was!' said Rishaan, heading to the bathroom.

Diya too quickly excused herself on the pretext of changing into home clothes.

On one hand, Kiara was upset with herself for her own behaviour, on the other, she wondered why she had begun to get this feeling of things not being right around her.

That night when Rishaan and Kiara lay on bed, the

bitterness caused by Kiara's words kept playing on Rishaan's mind.

'Rishaan, are you still upset about what I said?' Kiara asked him, holding his hand.

Rishaan ignored her.

'Rishaan, you know how much I love you.'

'Do you trust me?' Rishaan asked her.

'Yes and no. Not quite,' is what Kiara had almost said, until she realized that she actually did not know what to say. She simply nodded in confusion.

'Well, then chill and sleep peacefully,' Rishaan told her in an affectionately chiding tone.

'I hope you are coming to Goa?' she asked him.

'Yes. Unless you don't want me to...'

'Huh! So the writer has started playing with words. You are most welcome, Rishaan; unless you have other 'scripting' plans,' she said, sarcastically.

'I don't. I am all yours, except that in Goa I would like to take a few hours off to meet a friend,' he replied. 'But are you sure you want Diya to join us?' he added, rather pointedly.

Kiara nodded, not meaning to upset the status quo, even though she wasn't particularly excited anymore about the prospect of Diya accompanying them.

Half an hour later when Rishaan had fallen asleep or so it seemed, Kiara went to Diya's room. Holding a pen and paper in her hands, Diya looked rather lost. She kept thinking about the two days that she had spent with Rishaan, how she had ended up confiding in him her worst kept secret, his unusual interest in her and finally Kiara passing that snide remark that left both her and Rishaan awkward. It was only when Kiara called her name that Diya came ot of her reverie.

'Kiara, let me stay back in Mumbai. I will utilize these three days to hunt for an accommodation for myself,' Diya said.

'Relax darling. What's the hurry? You can do it after we return from Goa.'

'But Kiara, you and Rishaan anyway get very less time together. What's the point of me joining in and ruining all the fun?'

'Sweetheart, remember we had promised each other on our last Goa trip that we would come back to Goa together. I so want to spend some girlie time with you,' Kiara insisted.

'Are you sure?'

'Of course.'

After some more pursuing by Kiara, Diya relented on the condition that she would share the expenses of the trip.

Kiara agreed and the two hugged each other. Even as they hugged, Kiara's face held a mysterious smile.

Upon returning home early that evening, Kiara had found the door locked. She had enquired from the lift's watchmen as to how long Rishaan and Diya had been away.

'From the time you left. Rishaan bhaiya and that girl went out together, both yesterday and today,' the watchman had told her, rather snidely.

Kiara wanted the Goa trip to happen so that she could find out if all was indeed well between Rishaan and her. She wanted Goa to help her understand if there were any undercurrents she was unaware of.

Seventeen

You know when you're in love when you can't fall asleep because reality is finally better than your dreams.
—DR SEUSS

On their early morning flight from Mumbai to Goa, Diya occupied the window seat, Kiara the middle one and Rishaan the aisle side. Rishaan's previous three trips to Goa were full of joyous excitement. But this one was different. The excitement was mellowed; instead an air of unspoken tension loomed over the three of them. Rishaan had never seen Kiara this conscious before. In fact, ever since she returned from her Delhi trip, something seemed amiss. Had he indeed given her reasons to feel insecure?

Diya appeared lost and for most part of the journey looked out of the window, perhaps to escape awkward eye contacts. Kiara, who was running short of sleep, dozed off the moment their flight took off. All along the journey, she kept her hand on Rishaan's. Rishaan, for his part, remained wide awake, thinking about the last few days. He sure had a terrific film script out of Diya's life. But now, his interests had gone beyond the script. The character fascinated him so much that he craved to unravel more about her. His level of interest in Diya confounded him.

In the middle of the flight, Kiara woke up to go the washroom. When she returned, she was too lazy to push her way into the middle seat. And with Rishaan readily offering to shift seats, the seating arrangement changed. With 20 minutes still remaining for the flight to land, a sleep starved Kiara took another power nap, this time holding Rishaan's right hand more firmly. Rishaan's other hand, though, nervously moved to touch Diya's. Her heart skipped a beat. She pulled her hand away. But a defiant Rishaan held her wrist again, this time firmly and in a more friend-like manner. The changing behavioural dynamics between the three perhaps gave out a foreboding of what was to come in Goa.

When the flight landed at the Dabolim Airport, Rishaan felt very uncanny. Despite the vibrant greenery all around and the smell of the sea not too far away, all through their journey from the airport to their resort in Colva, the excitement in Rishaan seemed replaced by an unknown fear that he found very difficult to decipher.

Kiara and Diya spent the afternoon on a beach shack very close to their 4-star resort, while Rishaan spent his time in the resort room, flipping through the TV channels.

'It has been seven long years,' Kiara reminisced, sipping beer from her can. 'What a long journey it has been, Diya!'

Diya nodded.

'I am so glad we've fulfilled our promise of coming back to this Colva beach. There...that red flag over there in front of Bob's massage centre. That's where we had bumped into that gay firang,' Diya recalled, her efforts at sounding nostalgic clearly showing now.

'You were a hot chic then, babes,' laughed Kiara.

Diya did not know if it was a compliment or a rebuke. It seemed as if the next sentence that Kiara had in mind was, 'Not anymore, you ugly bitch.'

'Come let's take a walk along the beach,' suggested Kiara.

Diya was quite happy to do so, as their conversation lacked a natural flow.

By the evening, it was time for the sangeet ceremony of Kiara's friend, Anju. Anju was Kiara's classmate during her MBA in Pune. Her father owned a restaurant at Panjim, where they also lived. They had hired a sea-facing bungalow at the lovely Baga beach in north Goa for the wedding ceremony to take place. Nearly thirty friends of Kiara's were expected in Goa for the wedding. A few of them were married and most of them were in a relationship. Since, neither Rishaan nor Diya had any particular plans for the evening, they tagged along with Kiara.

'So is Ajit expected?' Rishaan asked Kiara, as they drove down to attend the sangeet.

'Yes, he is,' replied Kiara, somewhat curtly.

'And how long is the sangeet expected to last.'

'Can't say, Rishaan. Try and enjoy it for me.'

Rishaan could sense Kiara was upset with his rather detached behaviour. He held her hand affectionately, even though the gesture did not seem natural.

It hurt Kiara to think that Rishaan was not excited about attending their first wedding together as couple. She wanted to have a heart to heart chat with Rishaan. But that might have to wait till they reach Mumbai.

At the party, Kiara introduced Rishaan and Diya to all her friends. The only familiar faces that Rishaan could spot at the party were: Ajit, with whom he wasn't quite comfortable, given Ajit's history with Kiara, and a couple of Kiara's girl friends who had come to his place for a party. As for Diya, she knew nobody.

True to the spirit of the evening, Kiara and her gang of friends had taken to the dance floor. The DJ was playing an eclectic assortment of some of the best Hindi film numbers, both recent and retro. Soon Kiara took to drinking, given the company she was in.

Rishaan tried his best to put up with the loud music. But as usual, he couldn't sustain his pretence for long. He was and would always remain a loner. Diya, on the other hand, even though she tried chatting with two of Kiara's friends, found herself completely out of place.

With a glass of whisky in hand he walked outside to the garden. To his surprise, the garden opened into the sea beach. He went to the edge of the garden, sat on the wall and soaked in the lovely sea breeze. He loved the serenity that the sea shores provided.

'Rishaan,' a voice called from behind.

He was happy to see that it was Diya. Holding a glass of coke in her hand, her elegant white dress looked strikingly pretty in the darkness.

'Hey Diya, aren't you enjoying the dance?'

'Well, not quite,' she smiled.

Two lonely souls thus found good company for the evening and ended opening up more that they would have otherwise in Mumbai.

'Diya, despite all that you've gone through, it's so amazing that you are still so optimistic about life,' said Rishaan. 'Do you aspire to fall in love again?'

Rishaan had presumed what the answer would be. So when she shook her head in denial assertively, it rattled Rishaan.

'A woman can be complete without a man. At least, I don't think I need a man to be happy.'

The answer disappointed Rishaan. His interest in Diya had begun to make him feel possessive about her.

While Rishaan and Diya were chatting in the garden, Kiara and Ajit came out of the dance floor to the first floor balcony for a brief chat. Ajit had been meaning to tell her everything about his Chinese fiancé. The moment Kiara entered the balcony, she saw Rishaan and Diya sitting together at the far end of the solitary garden. Even though she heard Ajit out, she remained distracted looking towards Rishaan and Diya.

'Rishaan, can I ask you something?' asked Diya. 'Why do I see melancholy in you? I mean, you have every reason to be happy. You are getting to pursue a career you wanted. You have a girlfriend who loves you. Why then do I find you this lonely?'

Rishaan smiled uncomfortably, not knowing how to deal with a the touchy query.

'I am happy, Diya. I am quite happy.'

'Sure?'

Rishaan nodded. His nod lacked confidence. A brief pause preceded Diya's next query.

'Do you love Kiara?'

Rishaan hated Diya for asking him this question. Why

did every woman expect a man to have a clear answer to something as abstract as love? What is love? Isn't loving someone different from falling in love?

'I love Kiara. But I am not in love with her,' Rishaan attempted to answer.

'You do not always need to play with words, Mr Writer.'

'I don't,' Rishaan asserted.

He excused himself on the pretext of refilling a drink. Sitting alone, Diya kept pondering over his words: 'I love Kiara. But I am not in love with her.' Was Rishaan's not being in love with Kiara and his unusual interest in her linked? As she spent some lonely moments looking into the sea, she told herself that she would shift out of Kiara's house at the earliest possible. She already had enough complications in her life to deal with; she could not afford any more.

When Rishaan entered the party area, he could not find Kiara. On asking one of her friends, he was guided to the balcony where he was surprised to see Kiara and Ajit gossiping alone. Ajit had been telling her something confidential and seeing Rishaan there, he stopped at once.

'Oh I'm sorry. You guys can carry on your private talk,' said Rishaan, sounding acerbic.

'Oh common, Rishaan. Ajit was just telling me about his latest girlfriend,' Kiara explained. 'By the way, why is your glass empty? Give, I'll get you a refill.'

Kiara left, leaving Ajit and Rishaan alone.

'Congrats, dude! At a time when the Chinese are getting more and more aggressive on the Indian border, you seem to know how to tame them. Cheers on your Chinese girlfriend,' Rishaan exclaimed, rather wryly.

'Rishaan, you know what, Indian girls prefer good guys like you. No wonder then that a haraami like me has to scout for girls abroad,' said Ajit, laughing alone at his own joke.

Rishaan did not like his riposte. Even as Kiara came and handed him his glass of whisky, he seethed in anger thinking that a self-professed haraami like Ajit was once Kiara's boyfriend.

He spent the rest of the evening chatting with Diya. He was careful and conscious with his words to ensure that the only person he felt comfortable talking to at the party, was in no way inconvenienced by the chaos brewing in his head.

It was 3.30 in the morning when Rishaan, Kiara and Diya reached their resort. While Kiara slept till late, Rishaan was up by 7. He took a long walk on the empty beach, trying to decipher his unusual propensities. Was he falling in love all over again? Or was he finally falling in love now? His restlessness and anxieties were perhaps hinting at a life-altering development. Just that, he wasn't sure if he was indeed prepared for one.

He tried to calm himself, sipping coconut water. And then typed a message for Diya, *Diya, pls pls stay back in the hotel today. I want to discuss the script with you.*

Diya, awoken by the sound of the incoming message, had a sense of where his supposed 'script' was going. Surprisingly, the situation did not repulse her as much as she had thought it would. Yes, she had begun to like his company. But she couldn't foresee the repercussions of Rishaan's unusual fondness. Maybe she was confident that she could handle it, considering she had closed herself to men. But was Rishaan equipped to handle the situation?

Bad idea. We must go with Kiara. She typed back.

Bad idea. Trust me, we'll again get bored to death there. He wrote back.

For the next 10 minutes, there was no reply. Getting more audacious, Rishaan typed out the plan in his next message.

Just pretend you have sprained your leg and can't step out today. Rest I'll handle.

For the next few minutes there was again no response. Tired of whiling away his time, Rishaan walked back to the resort room. The sound of him opening the door woke up Kiara. Still clinging to her pillow and rubbing her eyes, she asked him, 'Rishaan, where were you? Come here baby.' Kiara, who seemed to be in a romantic mood, pulled him into the bed and rolled over him clasped his body with hers. Just then, he received a message.

'Your phone rings at all the wrong times,' she teased, holding out the cell to him. 'I'll just pee and come.'

Left alone, Rishaan opened to read the message.

Okay, was the cryptic message from Diya.

He looked rather confused thinking about the complex situations that were building around him. With the day having just begun, he knew it could well be a day like no other.

Eighteen

A relationship is not a test.
So why cheat?

Fourteen hours later, Rishaan and Diya found themselves all alone at the classy Oriental Restaurant of the Resort. It was drizzling outside interspersed with ominous sounds of thunderous cloudbursts. Both of them seemed confused and uncertain about everything. The way things had unexpectedly transpired in the last few hours, it had left both Rishaan and Diya digging for many answers.

Diya had pretended to have sprained her leg and hence stayed back in the room to rest. Rishaan pretended that he was going to meet his friend at Madgaon.

'Had Diya also begun to feel for him like he did for her?' Rishaan wondered. 'And what exactly do I feel for her? Infatuation? Fondness? Love?'

'What is this guy really upto? He probably does not love Kiara? Has he, by any chance, begun to love me?' Diya dreaded.

The mutual confusion thwarted smooth conversation,

until Diya decided that she had to set the record straight. She better do it before it's too late.

'Rishaan, I want to tell you something,' she said purposefully. Rishaan felt somewhat relieved, hoping her words might provide more clarity about the situation they found themselves entangled in.

'Rishaan, you know, as sensitive and romantic individuals, it's not entirely unnatural for us to feel attracted to people outside the conventional arrangements that we live in,' Diya tried explaining, although struggling with her thoughts and words. 'I don't want to flatter myself by thinking you are attracted to me; rather I'd believe we are drawn to each other. But at least for me, it all ends here. That's about all that I have to offer to you: companionship, conversation and company. I couldn't have taken it any further even if you were not my best friend's boyfriend.'

'Ah...w...well...I don't know what to say, Diya. But are you not being too hard on yourself?'

'Rishaan, after what I have gone through in life, I have decided I will never allow a man a stake in my life. In fact, that's the reason I wanted to meet you. I had to tell you two things.'

Rishaan looked in anticipation, wondering what he would discover now.

'The first bit might help you in your script because it's about me, that part of me, which I am still not ready to share with the world. Rishaan, apart from the book that I am working on, there's something else that is on my agenda immediately after that.'

'And what's it?'

A pregnant, still pause preceded her answer.

'I want to be a mother, a single mother.'

The sentence numbed Rishaan. From all that he had known of her, he knew that she was braver than most other women he had known. But was this indeed bravery? Or was it plain rebellion? So what if she had had a heart-wrenching experience. She was still quite young. She could start afresh.

Diya spelt out her thoughts further. Given that she had started planning her life ahead, surrogate motherhood was well thought out in her scheme of things. Artificial insemination is the way she planned to make it happen. Diya's conviction shocked Rishaan.

'I wanted you to know this because though my book will end before I reach that chapter, but the story of my life will perhaps remain incomplete until I live that experience.'

'Are you indeed sure about it?' Rishaan asked her, looking dazed by her conviction.

'I am as sure about it as I am about the fact that this conversation is indeed happening between us.'

Rishaan hugged her, the profound feelings that he had developed for her, making the hug more intimate than it would have been otherwise.

'What's the other thing that you wanted to tell me?' he asked her.

'That I will be shifting out of your place as soon as possible, and that we would never meet in Kiara's absence again.'

Given the assertive tenor that Diya had maintained throughout the evening, Rishaan didn't have much option other than nodding in acquiescence. Diya also had a word of advice for Rishaan, 'Take your time, chat with Kiara about your issues, if it doesn't work out then leave it. But be transparent and honest about the whole thing.'

◆

Even as Kiara witnessed Anju and her groom taking the saat pheras, she looked distracted and lost. She continued showering petals at the bride and groom even after the ritual was over. Ajit saw her and knew something was amiss.

'Something is not right between Rishaan and me...' she confided to Ajit and added after a pause, 'why do I get the impression that he and Diya are having a scene?'

◆

As Rishaan and Diya sat at the dimly lit restaurant sipping wine, Rishaan felt a sinking feeling settling in his chest. He knew that these were the last few hours that he was spending with the very first girl he had actually fallen in love with. The romantic in him wanted adventure instead of sedentary conversation. The drizzle had stopped by now, making the breezy weather seem more tempting than ever.

'A scooter ride?' He asked her.

Given the clarity in her thought, Diya agreed.

Hiring a rented scooter Rishaan drove Diya to a small hilltop that overlooked the Colva beach. It was a place, as tranquil and romantic as any they could find in the whole of Goa.

'I discovered this hidden paradise when I had come to Goa two years ago with my office friends. We had camped here the whole night. And mind you, it was the most awesome experience of our lives.'

Rishaan was tempted to watch the sunrise at the hilltop once again. But he knew that was wishful thinking. He held Diya's hand and took her to the edge of the cliff. Holding each other's hands, they absorbed the beatific sea breeze, with the sound of the waves crashing on the rocks below making the experience all the more majestic.

As they lived this moment to the fullest, Diya realized that she was not as strong as she pretended to be. She still had a heart, which at times beat faster than it normally did. She still had a life that could not evacuate all men out of it. She still had hormones that were not immune to the effects of attraction to the opposite sex.

Alas, she also had a conscience that would not permit her to indulge in anything which she found unethical.

At this point, a sudden gush of rain intervened to prevent what could have been a moment Diya would have regretted all her life. The rains made them end their hilltop rendezvous rather abruptly. Rishaan drove Diya back to the hotel.

Half an hour later, they met again at the Oriental restaurant for a quick dinner. By now, it was quite empty. After placing their orders, as they waited for the food to be served, they were taken in by the lovely Mozart symphony playing in the backdrop. The dim but elegant lighting only complemented the music all too well.

Thirsting for more excitement, Rishaan held Diya's hand and led her to dance with him in the vacant centre of the hall. Initially she felt a bit awkward, until she completely gave in to the soulful music. They danced in flow as naturally as though they had been doing it all their lives, unmindful of the world outside. When the music ended, they found themselves uncomfortably close to each other, with barely a few inches separating their lips. They stood in that volatile position for some time, unsure whether to surge ahead or to retreat. Rishaan, notwithstanding his impulses, planted a dry kiss on her lips. Diya's lips allowed him the leeway, her shut eyes only reflecting her acute dilemma.

It was only when Rishaan retreated that Diya realized that the defence she had carefully constructed all around her, had crumbled. She hated herself for betraying her best friend. She bolted out of the hall and shut herself in her room. Rishaan, for his part, battled a wide gamut of emotions. He hated the situation he was in: a fiancé he struggled to love and the fiancé's best friend he could not prevent himself from loving.

Hassled, he walked to and fro in the resort garden, just outside the reception area, when the piercing headlights of an SUV flashed on his face. Ajit was at the driver's seat. He had come to drop Kiara. With the lights focused directly on Rishaan's face, Kiara could see that he was troubled. It was high time she figured him out.

◆

That night, much after Rishaan had dozed off, Kiara remained awake late into the night. A gamut of images from the last few weeks swamped her mind: of Rishaan and Diya practising yoga together, of them spending hours at the Madh resort, of them all by themselves at the sangeet ceremony and then bunking the wedding to spend time together. All these incidences coincided with Rishaan's growing detachment with Kiara. He had almost stopped behaving like her boyfriend at times. Leave alone sex, which was once the most compelling part of their relationship, even simple gestures like holding hands and planting impromptu kisses seemed to have become a thing of the past. Kiara wanted to know what was in his mind. She felt more restless than ever to decode him.

After spending a couple of restless hours turning sides on the bed, battling for sleep, Kiara finally got up and stepped out of the room. She went to the reception, woke up the reception manager and doled out a 1,000 rupees note to him.

Half an hour later, she sat at the hotel office viewing the CCTV footage of the Oriental Cuisine Restaurant, where Rishaan and Diya had spent the entire evening together. She tried hard to keep herself calm as the visuals only corroborated her worst fears. She knew now why her boyfriend had been behaving less like one, lately.

Next morning, Kiara conjured an excited visage to conceal the angst inside. She mooted a plan for the three of them to indulge in some wild beach fun, before they boarded their flight back to Mumbai in the evening. Rishaan found Kiara's sudden excitement a bit strange, but attributed it to her whimsical, temperamental nature.

As the ladies took their time to get ready, Rishaan headed to the beach alone, carrying his camera. Kiara assured him that she and Diya would join him at the beach soon.

Kiara then went to Diya's room and held out a packet to her.

'What is this?' Diya asked.

'Take a look.'

To Diya's surprise, it was a bikini. It was the same polka dot bikini which Rishaan had gifted Kiara when he proposed her.

'Come on babes, wear it. Let's have some real beach fun.

We might not come to Goa together again.'

Diya found Kiara's behaviour unusual and somewhat weird.

A few minutes later, Diya and Kiara reached the beach in their sleeveless tops and shorts. Rishaan, who was wearing just his Bermuda shorts and clicking some landscape pictures, found their revived girlie camaraderie a bit difficult to digest. Had Kiara got wind of what had transpired between him and Diya the previous evening? Kiara suddenly seemed a bit too relaxed and jovial.

Rishaan, at this point, had no idea of the surprise that Kiara was about to spring at him. Kiara took off her shorts and top and then persuaded a sheepish Diya to do the same. Rishaan stood dazed at the sight of two extremely gorgeous women standing right in front of him in scintillating bikinis. He was baffled to find Diya wearing the same polka dot bikini that he had gifted to Kiara.

'Doesn't Diya look mind-blowing in this bikini?' Kiara asked him, purposely putting him in an awkward spot.

He wondered what Kiara was trying to do? If she was trying to test his loyalty, this really wasn't the best way to do it.

'Come on, Rish. Click us together.'

Saying this, Kiara made Diya pose with her. With unsure expressions that made her look really nervous, Diya's awkwardness was apparent.

'Come on, babes. What's bothering you? Why can't you be like we were in college, absolutely bindaas?' Kiara chided her.

There, on the beach, the two struck some scintillating poses, making Rishaan skip a beat or two. He found the situation very strange; on the one hand, he couldn't be luckier than this to be clicking two extremely irresistible women posing in just their three triangles; on the other, he had an eerie feeling that a massive explosion was about to happen.

As Kiara made Diya strike different poses with her, Diya could feel Kiara handling her in a rather rough, unaffectionate way. Diya knew this was not Kiara's normal behaviour. There was something that was really bugging her. Diya had no idea know what it could be.

'Rishaan, tell me who looks more gorgeous, Diya or I?' Kiara asked him teasingly, deriving some sort of sadistic pleasure in seeing him struggle for answer.

'Say Rishaan,' she exhorted him.

'Both.'

'That's not fair.'

'Diya,' he said, conveniently hiding his face behind the camera lense.

'Of course! My friend is the most gorgeous woman in the world,' Kiara said, sounding more bitter than ever.

Done with their share of pictures, Kiara snatched the camera from Rishaan.

'Come on guys, now you two pose together. It's my time to click pictures. Come on Rishaan, you look like such a beach bum,' said Kiara, forcefully pushing the two towards each other.

This really put Rishaan and Diya in a very uncomfortable spot.

'Come on Rishaan, be a sport. Come on, Diya babes.'

Rishaan couldn't believe what was happening to him. For a moment, he almost felt he and Diya were shooting a film. The very next, he so wanted this moment to be for real.

Yes, he was in love with Diya. He wanted Diya and him to be marooned on an island all alone, with no Kiara watching over them.

'Come on, get close. Rishaan, put your arms around her shoulder.'

Kiara clicked Rishaan and Diya in a seemingly dangerous pose. Rishaan silently enjoyed the moment, but Diya hated it. It made her feel like a whore.

'Wow! You guys look so good together,' raved Kiara, her tone getting bitterer with each passing moment.

'Kiara, I hope we are done,' Diya finally seemed to put her foot down on the nonsense.

'Wait darling. I need a picture of you guys kissing each other.'

'What! Are you out of your senses?' Diya lashed out at her friend.

'Come on, kiss each other. I want to take a shot.' Kiara remained firm. She moved towards them and held the camera very close to their faces.

'Come on, do it,' she reiterated.

'You've lost it, Kiara. You have completely lost it,' Diya snubbed her.

Kiara put the camera away, looked straight into Diya's eyes as if challenging her and in a moment, slapped her hard on the face.

'Bloody bitch. Is this what I get for all that I have done for you? Didn't you allow Rishaan to kiss you last evening?'

'Kiara, it's nothing like that. I have a safe conscience. I'll explain everything to you,' Diya tried reasoning with her.

Kiara planted another tight slap on her cheek.

'You have backstabbed me, Diya. It's not only about that one moment that was captured on the camera. I have been sensing something amiss between the two of you since the last two weeks. I am glad I found out that I wasn't hallucinating. I am glad I have discovered the truth.'

Shattered and embarrassed, Diya fled from there. Now it was just Kiara and Rishaan.

'Rishaan, you have killed my faith. You have killed whatever little belief I had in the word called love. I hate you, you cheater.'

Kiara was hopelessly devastated by now. She broke down and fell on her knees. Rishaan tried holding her, but she would not let him touch her.

'Get lost, Rishaan. Just leave me alone. Go from here.'

Rishaan stood by her side, helpless and laden with guilt, making frantic pleadings to calm her down. The paradise which Kiara was so diligently trying to build around her was mired by countless troubles. Kiara wondered whether she was simply unworthy of true love.

After half an hour of incessant crying when Kiara's tears seemed to have dried up, Rishaan finally managed to hold her hand and take her to the resort. He felt bad for Kiara. But in a true sense, it was Diya who occupied his thoughts and for whom he was really worried.

Nineteen

> *Love is so short, forgetting is so long.*
> —PABLO NERUDA

March 2014, United States

At the stroke of midnight, when frost seemed to have enveloped the entire area, Rishaan lit the funeral pyre of Diya, in a desolate Hindu crematorium almost 25 kilometres away from where she had been living in Bradford. She had succumbed to her injuries, barely a couple of hours before Rishaan reached the hospital. The 72-year-old Ian Robinson, in whose house Diya had stayed as a paying guest, stood by Rishaan's side, giving him support.

It was the most heart-wrenching moment for Rishaan. In the last three and half years, he had no clue where Diya was. He had absolutely no idea that he would meet her in a situation as cruel as this one. As Rishaan witnessed Diya's body turn to ashes, he couldn't help but feel guilty for her plight. A gamut of memories of the two months that she had spent with them thronged his mind. Had he failed her?

Rishaan was on the verge of collapsing when the

septuagenarian Robinson held him and put him in his car. Robinson drove him to his home, battling frost-hit low visibility and Rishaan's traumatized condition. It took them nearly an hour and half to reach home with Rishaan sitting dazed and lost in remorse all through the journey.

At 3 in the morning, they finally reached home. It was a large castle-shaped bungalow.

'Come,' Robinson guided Rishaan in.

As they sat in the living room by the bonfire, Robinson seemed a bit spaced out. He kept looking at the dazed Rishaan, as if wondering how to tell him what he had to. Eventually, he patted Rishaan's shoulder supportively, and instructed Rishaan to follow him to one of his inside rooms.

As Robinson opened the door, Rishaan saw a beautiful three-year-old angel peacefully sleeping on the bed. Rishaan was surprised to see this Indian looking kid.

'Diya's daughter,' Robinson said, in a hoarse, punctuated tenor.

The little angel was completely oblivious to the fact that her mother had departed leaving her alone to live all by herself.

From a wooden drawer, next to the bed, Robinson took out a piece of paper and handed it over to Rishaan.

'Diya was intuitive. I think she had foreseen her death. She had no other reason to write this letter just a month ago. She had asked me to send it to you and Kiara in case something happened to her.'

Robinson's words gave Rishaan goose bumps. What could the letter contain?

Rishaan stretched a trembling hand for the letter and started to read what he suspected could alter his life irreversibly.

Twenty

Being deeply loved by someone gives you strength, while loving someone deeply gives you courage.
—LAO TZU

September, 2010

The Goa trip had left Kiara devastated, Rishaan rattled and Diya shutting herself off from the world. Kiara wondered why she always suffered in love. Rishaan wondered why his quest for the perfect woman had to compulsively border upon utopia? Diya wondered why she couldn't stop herself from getting entangled in other people's agenda?

They were all flawed beings after all, much like everybody else in the universe.

After travelling back to Mumbai in a separate flight, Diya shifted out of Kiara's house within a day. She moved into a rental accommodation which she found on the internet, and where she somehow managed to convince the landlord to allow her to shift immediately, even before the registration formalities were complete. Diya did not give her new address to anybody. It was sheer coincidence that on the day she shifted into her new house, one of the private schools where she had applied for a job, called her for an interview and then immediately asked her to join the school as Counsellor Psychologist. She heaved a huge sigh of relief on receiving the offer letter.

She immediately changed her phone number and ended all ties with Kiara and Rishaan.

With Diya out of the picture, it was imminent for Kiara and Rishaan to decide their next step. They had been living in separate rooms and talking only when absolutely necessary, that too in monosyllables. Rishaan had tried talking to Kiara, but she was just not interested. Kiara was actually exploring the option of quitting her job and the city altogether. With two successive relationship disasters, the city seemed to be jinxed for her.

In this situation, one night, Rishaan caught up with his tomboyish ex-boss, Mita, over a drink. Ironic as it may seem, he felt Mita, who was unapologetically single after a string of relationship goof-ups, might be able to provide him a better insight than others. Having been briefed already on the phone by Rishaan, Mita had a fair idea of the problem between him and Kiara.

With a glass of whisky in her hand, Mita came straight to the point.

'So tell me dude, where does it stand at the moment?'

'Well, Kiara is planning to quit her job and go back to live with her mom in Delhi.' He added in an afterthought, 'But I think she still loves me. I can see it in her eyes. The reflection of hurt in her eyes haunts me.'

'Hmm... What about you? Are you prepared to accept your

mistake and seek her forgiveness?' Mita asked him.

'I am not sure. I would like to mend things between us. But I am afraid I might fail her again. I am just too confused.'

Rishaan sounded hopelessly hassled. Mita heard him out patiently, and gave a good thought to the situation before spelling out her mandate.

'I think you should go back to Kiara. Go to her, apologize profusely and ask for forgiveness.'

The advice startled Rishaan as Mita explained her viewpoint.

'You know what dude, getting attracted towards something that's forbidden, is the commonest human behaviour. You will experience that all your life, even more after you are married because marriage binds you and human nature hates bondage.' Rishaan heard her out carefully. 'Does getting attracted to someone else mean you don't love your girlfriend or your wife? Come on dude, as an evolved being, draw the line between infatuation and relationship. And if that doesn't make sense, just tell yourself that it's always good to spend your life with someone who loves you more than you love her. Go for Kiara!'

Mita's words kept resonating in Rishaan's ears much after he had returned home. It surprised him to think how the same woman, whom he found so irritating as a boss, could drill sense into his head. Had Mita changed? Or had his way of looking at her changed? He surmised that it was perhaps the latter.

Two days later, when Kiara came back from office, Rishaan surprised her by bending on his knees and unconditionally apologizing and pleading for forgiveness.

'Kiara, I allowed myself to get carried away. I committed a blunder by betraying your faith. I am really sorry.'

Kiara eventually forgave him, although the hurt persisted. The relationship just couldn't be like what it had been before Diya entered their lives.

It was only when Kiara and Rishaan began living being boyfriend and girlfriend a second time that Rishaan realized that the magic of their first innings could perhaps never be revived. At most, they could be good friends, which was not a bad deal considering it was friendship more than sex that sustained a relationship in the long run.

Two months went by. Rishaan and Kiara, slowly but steadily, had begun to pick the threads of their relationship. They had lowered their expectations from each other, which in turn helped them avoid disappointments. They had begun to give each other more space and seemed more at peace with each other's habits. But the magic of yore was gone! They had anyway begun to believe that the elusive magic was illusory; what was real was the companionship which had finally begun building up between them. Life seemed okay, though a tad boring.

For a change, Kiara took three weeks off to be with her mom. Together, they had planned to go on an excursion to Ladakh. Rishaan thought Kiara's absence would help him view things more objectively. To his surprise, he did not miss Kiara as much as he had expected to. In his heart of hearts, he wasn't closed to the idea of getting married to Kiara the next year. Perhaps marriage was the way to end all confusion. In a week's time, Rishaan got the news that his colleague and good friend from Star, Sudesh, had become a father. Since he was in between scripts and had free time to spare, he dropped in to pay a visit to the newborn in the suburban hospital. While leaving from the hospital, he saw someone that left him completely befuddled: a girl, who looked very much like Diya, walked out of the Assisted Reproductive Technology (ART) section. The girl briskly walked towards the exit door. He followed her, just to be doubly sure that the girl was Diya. To his shock, it indeed was her.

'Diya,' he called from behind.

Diya turned around at the direction of the voice. However, upon seeing Rishaan, she hastily rushed away, making sure she avoided him altogether. This entire bit left Rishaan completely confused. He turned back and saw a lady doctor come out of the ART section. As the doctor headed towards the maternity ward, Rishaan's friend, who was coming out of the ward, greeted the doctor warmly. The doctor seemed to know Rishaan's friend and exchanged a word with him before proceeding to work.

Rishaan hated to think what could have brought Diya to the hospital. It reminded him of their conversation in Goa where Diya had confessed of wanting to be surrogate mother. Had Diya indeed embarked upon doing the unthinkable?

◆

Around 11.30 in the night, as Diya read through her manuscript which was now complete, her doorbell rang. She tried seeing through the peeping glass, but could not see clearly as it was filled with dust.

She opened the door to get the shock of her life. Rishaan stood there, looking at her with yearning eyes. She didn't find it right to invite him in, nor could she get herself to shut the door on his face.

'Why are you complicating your life further?' Rishaan asked her possessively. 'Why the hell do you need to go for artificial insemination?'

A few minutes later, they sat in her living room, discussing about it.

'I need to do this to move to the next chapter of my life. And since I won't allow a man to be a stakeholder in my life, this is my way forward.'

Rishaan found her conviction frightening. Why did she have to be a compulsive maverick? Or was that the life that seemed most natural to her?

As Rishaan sat in Diya's room, disoriented and with little clarity on what had brought him there, he also wondered what was it that offended him most about her idea of going in for artificial insemination. Was he principally opposed to the thought of an unmarried woman wanting to become a mother in this manner? Or was he still possessive about her?

After chatting a bit about her work and life, Rishaan looked came to the point.

'Diya, I...I wanted to ask you something?' he spoke hesitantly and fumbling with words.

'Diya, can I be your sperm donor?' he asked, gathering himself and finally managing to look into her eyes.

The query jolted Diya. It left her numb. For a moment she wanted to believe those words had not been uttered at all. But alas, they were.

'Diya?' he said pleadingly, almost nudging her for an answer.

'No Rishaan. You can't.' She asserted, trying to muster all her courage.

'Why?'

For a moment she seemed hesitant to answer, but then she did.

'Because I have fallen in love with you.'

Rishaan froze in his chair.

'If I did not love you, I wouldn't have stayed back at the Goa resort with you. If I didn't, I wouldn't have gone for a scooter ride with you,' she said, trying hard to combat her emotions.

Diya's words left Rishaan baffled and perplexed. He looked stumped at the puzzles that life never ceased to throw up.

'In that case, isn't that all the more reason for me to be the donor?' he tried reasoning.

'That's precisely the reason why I don't want you to be the donor. You won't be able to keep yourself away from me or the baby, complicating many lives in the process,' Diya remained firm and unrelenting.

Rishaan hugged Diya tight before leaving for home.

As Rishaan drove back home, Diya's words kept resonating in his mind 'Because I have fallen in love with you. If I hadn't, I wouldn't have stayed back at the Goa resort with you.' Had he completely misread the situation? Had he lost a rare opportunity of finding true love?

Half an hour later when Diya was about to hit the bed, her doorbell rang again. She opened it, not quite alert about who it might be. Did she know it would be Rishaan? Rishaan looked at her with intensely passionate eyes which left nothing to be spoken. He embraced her and moved his lips very close to hers. He kissed her passionately. Diya reciprocated with the same alacrity and intensity. Within minutes, they made love as if they were born to make love to each other. They loved each other like there was no tomorrow. Rishaan and Diya were truly, madly, deeply in love with each other.

Rishaan and Diya remained awake for the rest of the night, just holding each other in a tight embrace. Myraid thoughts, dilemmas and fears invaded their minds. In the midst of all the chaos, their equanimity was quite impressive.

It was around 5 in the morning when Rishaan fell asleep. Diya, though, remained awake. At 7:30 or so, Diya heard Rishaan's cellphone vibrate repeatedly. She took a look at the screen only to find Kiara's name flashing on it. It made Diya feel miserable as she feared the worst to happen. Did Kiara somehow get to know of what had transpired between her and Rishaan last night? Would she ever be able to face Kiara again?

By the time Rishaan woke up, Kiara had already made up her mind. She had more or less decided her next course of action.

Half an hour later when Rishaan woke up, he was shocked to find seventeen missed calls from Kiara. He feared the worst but not of the nature it turned out to be. Kiara's mom had collapsed in their resort at Nainital the previous night. She was vomiting blood. They rushed her to Delhi by an air-ambulance and got her admitted at the Apollo Hospital.

Rishaan was aghast. He wondered how life could be this unpredictable. The earth-shattering developments of the last few hours had surely turned his life topsy-turvy.

A few hours later Rishaan stood outside the ICU of the Apollo Hospital in Delhi giving Kiara the much needed support. Kiara was inconsolable.

'I just can't afford to lose Mom. She's my anchor, she's my everything.'

As Rishaan held Kiara supportively, her body leaning against his, he couldn't hold back his emotions. He burst into tears and broke down in the hospital itself. Why was life testing him like this? Rishaan could not tell Kiara the other half of his dilemma. Nonetheless, Kiara too hugged him tight.

Two days later when Kiara's Mom's reports came out, they corroborated Kiara's worst fears—her mom was suffering from an advanced stage of blood cancer and chances of her survival were slim.

Kiara was deeply disturbed by the ill news. She would hardly eat or sleep, and would remain tensed throughout. Rishaan, who had always seen Kiara as a strong, self-sufficient girl, found it miserable to see her in this condition. Apart from feeling guilty, he felt protective for her. For the next two weeks, he took good care of her like a father would have taken care of his kid in such a situation of despair.

Diya, who had not been in touch with Kiara ever since the Goa incident, left her a long message offering her prayers and good wishes for the speedy recovery of Kiara's mom. Diya also told her that she was always there for Kiara, if ever she needed help.

Two week later, when Kiara's Mom's was a bit better, Rishaan and Kiara brought the Mom to Mumbai and got her admitted to top cancer hospital in Bandra. For Rishaan, the last two weeks had been the worst phase of his life. In all the turbulence that had engulfed his life these last two weeks, he was forced to abandon the thoughts of that fateful night which had preceded his journey to Delhi. He wondered where he stood in the present situation. Did he still love Diya? Or was he already Kiara's husband? He knew that circumstances demanded of him to be the latter. If he chose otherwise, he'd hate himself for not standing by the woman who loved him. In any case, seeing Kiara in this fragile state, it was not possible for him to leave her alone.

Rishaan had tried calling Diya a few times. He just wanted to talk to her once after what had happened between them. Strangely, her cell was switched off. He also left messages on her phone, but they never got delivered. After Kiara's mom was shifted to Mumbai, Kiara had started spending the nights at the hospital beside her mother. On one of those nights while driving back home Rishaan, on an impulse, went to Diya's house. With her cellphone switched off, he was really worried for her.

When he reached her flat, he found a big lock hanging on the door. Upon asking the neighbours, they informed him that Diya had vacated the place a week back.

'But where did she go?' Rishaan asked in desperation.

'She didn't tell us. But we can give your flat-owner's number. Maybe she might have told him.'

The landlord told Rishaan that Diya had gone abroad, and that he knew nothing more about her whereabouts. Rishaan looked at the lock on the door and sighed wearily. No, he wasn't ditching Kiara; not in her present fragile state and perhaps not later either. After all, she had stood by him despite his failings. His interest in meeting Diya, he thought, was to unravel the enigma that she was. Diya's sudden disappearance only intrigued and baffled him. 'Alas, she will always remain a mystery for me!' he said, and left for home.

The three months that Kiara's mom spent in the hospital was an eye-opener for Rishaan. It was the most traumatic phase of their lives, where they tried every possible cure for her mother. Even chemotherapy, supervised by one of Mumbai's best oncologists, showed only limited effects. In this phase, Rishaan saw an altogether different side to Kiara, something he would never have got to see in a normal situation.

Kiara was not selfish, not in the least. Rather, she selflessly set aside all her agendas to take care of her mother and Rishaan too. She made sure Rishaan's scriptwriting assignments and meetings weren't affected. For this, she quit her job and took the full responsibility of attending to her mother. Even when Kiara's experienced worst of pain, she dealt with it all alone since Rishaan had an important narration two days later. After seeing this side of Kiara, Rishaan had a change of heart and possibly a final one: he just couldn't commit the sin of leaving her. She needed his support and he'd provide it to her all out.

This strengthened the bond between Kiara and Rishaan like never before. After Rishaan's narration was done and he bagged the film, he came forth to share Kiara's responsibilities. He at times worked from the hospital, allowing Kiara to return home and rest for a bit.

Three months later, the doctors gave up on Kiara's mother. 'It is now a matter of some weeks...' the doctors told them. Since the Mom had once expressed her wish to Kiara that she'd like to die at home, Kiara being the dutiful daughter, made sure that her wish was lived up to.

Rishaan and Kiara happily inconvenienced themselves to let Kiara's mom celebrate her last few days at home. One day, when the Mom had a strange feeling that her end was round the corner, she reluctantly expressed her wish to be able see Kiara and Rishaan get married. And the very next morning, the two exchanged vows on their terrace, with just a dozen or so friends to witness their big moment. That very night, Kiara's mom passed away.

In the last three years, Kiara had been an unexpectedly good wife and Rishaan an unexpectedly good husband. As a married couple, the nature of their relationship had evolved with time. Sex was no longer the crucial propellant between the two; rather shared empathy, companionship and long conversations made the bond stronger and better.

In the last one year, of course, there was a shared passion which both of them lived day in and day out and which had got them even closer: the desire to have a baby.

◆

Diya, who was overcome with guilt, felt an urgent urge to escape Mumbai and the unsavoury situation she found herself trapped in. She went to Florida to be with her maasi. It was only after she reached Florida that she discovered, to her shock, that she was pregnant. Diya mulled over all the possible options, but first she had to decide whether she wanted to abort the foetus or go ahead with her pregnancy. The maverick in her opted for the latter. She also had to decide whether to inform Rishaan about it. She did not; deciding to fight her battles all alone.

A year later when her maasi relocated to Australia, Diya stayed back in the U.S. She found herself a job, a primary school teacher in Bradford, and soon shifted there. Ian

Robinson, who was one of the trustees of the school, had invited Diya and her four-month-old daughter to stay in his place as paying guests.

Twenty-one

The best love is the kind that awakens the soul; that makes us reach for more, that plants the fire in our hearts and brings peace to our minds. That's what I hope to give you forever.
— THE NOTEBOOK

March, 2014, United States

It was morning. Rishaan sat nervously on the dining table, biting his nails, feeling jittery. Robinson stepped in holding the two-and-a-half-year-old baby girl, Anhaita. She looked like the prettiest toddler he had ever seen. Her eyes seemed distinctly like his own, her nose identical to her mother's.

It was the most overwhelming moment for Rishaan to see his child stand right in front of his eyes. He couldn't believe what he saw. How could everything change so radically in a matter of a few hours? He couldn't believe that had become a father two and a half years ago. 'Why didn't Diya tell me about it?! And how would Kiara react to the situation?' He dreaded thinking about her reaction.

'Anhaita, that's your Dad,' Robinson guided the child.

Rishaan opened his arms to embrace her. To his pleasant surprise, Anhaita came to him rather willingly. As Rishaan hugged his daughter, caressing her hair affectionately, everything seemed incredible.

'Call it intuition, but Diya had been preparing herself to the thought that Anhaita's Dad will come to take her with him one day,' Robinson informed. 'I have told her that her mom will be away for a few months. She has gone to visit God.'

Robinson's last sentence shook Rishaan. Rishaan dreaded to think how Kiara would react to the situation. 'Will she ever be able to accept the situation?' He feared she might go into acute depression and harm herself.

Right at that point, Kiara called Rishaan. Rishaan moved away to take her call, aware that after this conversation, things might never remain the same between him and Kiara.

'Kiara, Di...Diya is no more,' he informed her in a choked, stuttering voice.

He just didn't know how to divulge the other information to her, which was way more deadly.

'Kiara, I want to tell you something,' he started off and then got cold feet. 'Listen, there's something urgent I need to attend to. I will call you later.'

He dreaded the thought of breaking the news to Kiara. He was scared to imagine her reaction to the whole situation.

'D...daddy,' the little girl called out to him, demanding his attention.

Rishaan spent most of the day just observing Anhaita. He was to fly back with her the next night. At the back of his mind he remained occupied with the worry of breaking the news to Kiara.

The next evening before setting off to the airport, he got on to the internet at Robinson's place and wrote a long mail to Kiara explaining everything that had happened in the last forty-eight hours. There was no other way he could convey the truth to her. And every moment that he withheld the truth from Kiara made him feel miserable. He had to tell her the truth sooner or later. After his cathartic recollection of that fateful night with Diya, Rishaan ended the mail saying, 'Kiara, I have nothing to offer to you but apologies. I know that might not suffice. It tears me apart to think that I have failed you. And hence, I will respect and support whatever decision you take after reading my mail.'

Rishaan's journey to India was the most stressful journey of his life. Even as he attended to Anahita as patiently as he could, Kiara was constantly in his thoughts. Has she read his mail yet? What would she feel reading his mail? He was scared thinking she might do something really bizarre or hurt herself.

After his 18-hour-flight landed in Mumbai, Rishaan wished that the remaining 45 minute journey to home to be even longer. He was scared to face Kiara.

When Rishaan rang the bell it was 5.40 a.m. Holding a sleepy and jet-lagged Anhaita in his arms, he was prepared for the worst. Kiara opened within a moment, as if she had been waiting for him. She looked terribly distraught. She had not slept or eaten from the time she read his mail.

'Kiara...' Rishaan tried saying something, but was stopped by her hand gesture.

To his shock, he found two large suitcases lying behind her.

'I am here just to make sure what you wrote in the mail

was true. I hoped against all odds that it was a cruel joke or maybe your email was hacked and somebody played a prank. But now, after seeing you... At least that part of me, which belonged to you, is dead.'

Kiara walked out on Rishaan. From his window as Rishaan saw Kiara push her stuff into a cab and leave, he felt the chilling forlornness of a bereaved man. He wept like a kid, until Anahita's innocent attempts to wipe his tears had him control himself.

Rishaan hugged Anahita as though wanting to hold on to what he could still call his own. Rishaan knew that irrespective of all that was happening in his life, he could not allow his daughter's life to be affected by any of it. It was his and only his responsibility to raise this withering angel into a strong woman.

As dawn broke and the first ray of light entered his room, looking at Anahita, Rishaan felt more confident to start his life anew.

◆

Two and a half months went by in no time. In these months, Rishaan took most of his time away from work to understand Anahita better. After all, being a single father, that too in the circumstances in which he had become one, was something he could have never imagined. He and Anahita had in fact gone on a two-week holiday to Mount Abu, where they spent their time together in the midst of mountains and greenery playing, chatting and doing all things sweet and beautiful. This trip cemented their bond, and gave Rishaan some sort of confidence that he could indeed be a single father for the rest of his life.

In this process, Rishaan's work suffered and he lost out on a couple of important projects. But he did not mind it. He was clear about the fact that Anhaita was most important to him.

Rishaan admitted Anahita in a premium junior school for her nursery. Her first day in school was obviously a very proud and emotional moment for Rishaan.

Rishaan readied Anahita all by himself. And just when he was to drive Anahita to school, his old Honda City decided to ditch him. With little time in hand, Rishaan had no option but to drop Anahita in an auto.

They reached school right on time. With tears in his eyes, he saw Anahita off. These two hours of separation were a test of his ability of staying away from his daughter.

And as he turned away, he bumped into the gorgeous Bollywood starlet Shreya Sen. Shreya had a guest appearance and an item number in the movie Rishaan had written for director Aakash Jha. Shreya's item number was among the sexiest that Bollywood had ever seen. Rishaan had met her before, twice during the shoot and once at the premiere party of the film. And in fact, the two had got along well with each other, but never kept in touch after that.

Shreya, a bohemian, had adopted a two-year-old baby boy. Being a single mother, she had come to drop her son to school. And what a surprise it was to meet Shreya here after so many years.

Rishaan and Shreya decided to hang out over coffee at a nearby Starbucks Cafe. As Shreya drove her magnificent Red Porsche with Rishaan seated by her side, Rishaan found it surprising how life never ceased to throw the most unexpected surprises at him. He couldn't believe he was actually bonding over a parenting chat with someone he considered to be among the most gorgeous women in the world.

Rishaan knew that life and Bollywood were indeed capable of throwing up some crazy surprises.